In Death Do Flowers Grow

In
Death
Do
Flowers
Grow

A novella

RD Pires

ISBN-13 978-1-7347495-4-0

A DARK ESTATE IN CAMDEN

The Garrick Estate has a much grander name than the house should promote. As far as dwellings in Camden go, there are many houses with more character, more rooms, or views that could take one's breath away. These houses have roofs that aren't missing shingles, paint that hasn't flaked away in shards as big as black birch leaves, and once-thriving gardens that haven't succumbed to dead brambles.

Of course, most of these homes haven't also sat abandoned for many, many years.

The estate sits nestled in the trees on a not-so-busy hillside. Though the gate is wide, ivy has overtaken the brick columns, and each of the two lanterns is so thoroughly masked that they're unlikely to shed any light come nightfall. Oddly enough, the wild plant matter does not encroach upon the black wrought-iron gates but arches over them—as if knowing the way in must stay clear. But even so, the entrance is extraordinarily easy to miss. Brielle would've completely driven past the estate were it not for the little pinprick in the middle of her forehead that made her check the overgrown portal in her rearview mirror.

She pulls her Volkswagen off the road.

Leaving the engine running, Brielle looks both ways before crossing the narrow street. She jogs back to the forlorn gateway, her curiosity piqued. It might be the place she came here to see, but there's no immediately visible evidence to confirm her suspicions. A more affluent design might have seen the name of the original family forged into the wrought-iron gates themselves, but this does not seem to be the case.

Then she rips a strand of ivy away from the right-hand column, and there's her proof: a modest oval plaque with the family name. Garrick.

Nodding pragmatically, she proceeds to pull on the gate. It doesn't budge, probably due to the shattered hinge she discovers, but her contact had assured her the way would be open. So, Brielle perseveres, and finds that if she lifts the gate, it opens quite readily.

When the way is cleared, Brielle wanders back to her car. The road is sufficiently narrow that she has to make a several-pointed star to U-turn, but luckily the late hour means that no other cars come her way. Then she drives up what was probably once a gravel lane but has now become an overgrown suggestion of a path pocked by divots and holes, which leads her to a circular driveway at the foot of the house.

As she parks her car, her phone rings. Brielle maneuvers in her seat to slip the phone out of her jacket pocket, but upon seeing her brother's name, she lets it go unanswered. She knows why Kam is calling. She'll call him back later. Right now, she wants to be in the moment. Right now, she needs her mind open and clear.

Time for her favorite part: the introduction.

Brielle steps out into the wintry night air. The road beyond the gate had been sheltered by foliage, but the house sits in an open field, and as such, a persistent, chilly breeze sweeps across the grounds. She hears rather than sees the tall grass rustling around her. In the distance, the silhouettes of trees bend this way and that. She treats this like a sort of welcome, as if each blade of grass and moaning limb is struggling to get a good look at her.

And then there's the looming house. This late in the evening, the details are difficult to make out, though it certainly looks like she would've expected: austerely beautiful but tragically rundown, a modicum of clashing, half-assed efforts to conjure elegance. What little she can see lacks the coherence of an artistic eye—filigree in odd places, siding that doesn't quite match. The one stand-out feature, however, is the large bay window to the left of the front door. She wishes she could see it all more clearly, but that will probably have to wait until morning.

Suddenly, the entire house is awash with light. For a maddening moment, Brielle wonders if maybe it read her mind, before she realizes it's just the headlights of another car coming up the drive. She smiles at her own mistake.

The second vehicle parks behind her own. Though the engine dies, the headlights stay lit, trained on the back of Brielle's Volkswagen and the overgrown border of the circular driveway. A short, heavyset woman emerges.

"Sorry I'm late," she says, sounding somewhat harried. "There was a mother deer and her two fawns blocking the road— positively *rampant* in this area. Honked and everything. They didn't care. I'm guessing you're Brielle?"

"At your service."

"I'm Nadine Toren," the woman says, revealing herself to be the current owner of the Garrick Estate and Brielle's point of contact. Brielle likes her jacket, which is made of a very soft-looking fleece depicting a pack of wolves roaming beneath a violet night sky. "To be honest, I was skeptical you'd get here so fast when you told me where you were coming from."

"My driving foot was leaden last night," Brielle says. Stepping nearer, she holds out her hand. Nadine complies with an abbreviated shake, though her grip is firm.

"Did you find the place no problem?"

"Yeah, it called to me." Brielle chuckles. "It is a bit hard to see though, isn't it."

"When it's ready I'll make the entrance more inviting, but I figured there are more pressing issues at the moment."

Nadine clears her throat, eyes shifting from Brielle to the house and back to Brielle again, never quite making direct contact.

"So," she says. "So."

"Do you live close by?" Brielle asks, prompting conversation. She's eager to begin. Is the woman always so skittish?

"Oh! Yes, I meant to give you my address." Nadine rummages through the pockets of her jacket and draws out a small slip of paper torn from a larger sheet. "In case you need anything. I'm just a few miles *that* way—big white house. Sometimes I think too big, you know?"

Brielle smiles appreciatively as she takes the slip of paper.

"I wonder why I don't just move, actually—somewhere smaller. But I've been there for seven years now. It feels wrong to leave."

"I know what you mean," Brielle says, even though she has never felt this way. "Can you tell me about this place?"

She nods toward the looming figure of the house behind them.

"Of course, of course," Nadine says. Her eyes lose focus as she sorts through the details. Brielle can't help but notice the woman's beauty—her features appear almost drawn, like the work of an artist's hand. Symmetrical. Full. Expressive. The way the headlights catch her brown skin makes her resemble more of a painting than a human being. "I lived in Portland for most of my life," she says finally. "But at a certain point—right around the time my marriage dissolved—I realized I didn't want to be there anymore. It'd been that way for a long time, but the thought never dawned on me that I could move. Don't ask me how. It doesn't make sense, looking back.

"The house I live in now was my grandparents' summer home, and they were kind enough to let me have it. That was supposed to be a temporary living situation, but it became one of those things—I just never moved out. There was no reason to." Brielle imagines being gifted a house. Though she's never been one to want something so permanent, she still recognizes the grandiosity.

"Shortly after gifting me the house, my grandfather passed away," Nadine says. "And my grandmother did the same a few years ago."

"I'm sorry for your loss," Brielle says.

Nadine nods her gratitude and shifts her weight to one hip, leaning against the hood of Brielle's car.

"We weren't particularly close in the end, but the loss was difficult."

"What about your parents?"

"They weren't in the picture much," Nadine says, and though her voice is level, there's a spiteful punctuation to her phrasing. "Anyway, when my grandparents died, they left me a sizable inheritance. Even in death they never stopped taking care of me. I recognize how lucky I've been."

"I know you said you never found a reason to leave, but is there any particular reason you stayed in that house? In Camden?"

"I love the trees," she says. "I love the seasons."

"I hear Maine can get pretty brutal."

"Anywhere can get 'pretty brutal' depending on what you're used to," Nadine counters.

"Fair enough. I'd like to return to my initial question though."

"And what was that?"

"Could you tell me about *this* house?"

"Right."

Nadine turns now to face the looming shadow.

"When I received the money, I bought the Garrick Estate with the intention of making it an inn," Nadine says in the same way a parent might talk while watching their child play, knowing the child is too engrossed in their own world to hear the adults discussing them. "I thought from the pictures that it just needed a little love and attention. I thought it might not be too hard to fix up. I like a good project, you see."

"But that's not the case?"

"No," she says flatly. "It isn't."

"Do you know the history of the estate?"

"Some say the Garrick family had it built in the eighteen hundreds, some say the early nineteen hundreds. It doesn't matter to me—it's old like everything else in this part of the country. Beyond that, I didn't inquire much. It's had its share of owners, like old houses do. Some who treated it well and others, I'm sure, who didn't want to put in the effort. Then in the 1960s, it became a bed and breakfast, and that's where things left off until me.

"I'd been living here for four years by the time I bought the house. The beauty of a town this size is that you can still be anonymous while knowing a lot of people. Friends, neighbors. Everyone is plenty nice once you get to know them. But as soon as I started telling people about my plans, I started getting funny looks. Anyone who'd been here long enough warned me of the same thing."

"Which is?"

"That the house is haunted."

Nadine and Brielle lock eyes.

"By who?" Brielle asks. "Or by what?"

"By ghosts," Nadine says simply. She shrugs. "They won't say any more than that."

"What evidence do they have?"

"Not much, to be honest. Nobody will go near it—not even the teenagers. But there have been reports of noises. Some say they've heard screams."

Brielle wants to roll her eyes, though she refrains out of courtesy. Screams are hardly evidence of anything besides squatters who don't want to be bothered. Still, it's not her business to doubt. It's her business to vanquish.

"So you don't know anything else about who's haunting the place?" she asks, hoping for a bit more to go on.

"I don't. I'm sorry." Nadine dons a grimace.

"Have you…never been inside?"

Nadine shakes her head, her expression somber.

"But you've owned it for three years?"

"I take the word of the folks who've been here," Nadine says, her voice low. "I believe them. I believe there are ghosts in there. I don't want to face that. But I'm hopeful, given your expertise, you can help me."

Brielle takes a moment to observe her surroundings again—the black line of trees in the distance, untamed weeds and grass grown wild everywhere, and the dark shadow of the house looming over them. If Nadine is so opposed to the uncanny, why had she ever sought to buy the Garrick Estate in the first place?

"I will do my best," Brielle says, focusing her attention back on her client.

Nadine sighs with relief. "I can't thank you enough. The sooner the better—not just so I can open the bed and breakfast, of course," she adds, lest Brielle think anything less of her for wanting to economically utilize her property. "I also think it's important to lay to rest any spirits that might be lingering."

Brielle raises an eyebrow. That isn't something clients often say—usually, they're tired of being frightened half to death and want to be left alone. As someone who has built a life setting trapped spirits free, Brielle appreciates the empathy it takes to show an ounce of concern for the souls of the dead, even if the woman is too skittish to have actually checked for them.

"Shall I start immediately then?"

FINDING A GHOST

A familiar dusty silence greets her inside the house: the type of dusty silence where more than air seems to fill the room. Cotton, perhaps—invisible and somehow breathable. Her ears ring with the silence, made unhappy by the lack of substance even though the soles of her shoes thud on the aging floorboards and the front door clicks shut behind her. She holds her breath, anxious to meet the house, and the house stares in at her with discerning anticipation.

"Tension" is the first word that comes to mind.

Perhaps it's the dark shadows, the deep corners, the details left to the imagination in the absence of light. She envisions taut strings crisscrossing the open air from one wall to another, holding everything together. If one should snap, then all hell might break loose. This is a classic haunted house vibe if ever she's been a part of one. Brielle admits that she finds this atmosphere pleasing, even if she can't completely rid herself of fear. The first night at any new haunting makes her feel most alive.

"Hello?" she asks the emptiness, wondering if the alleged ghosts can hear her. But there is no response.

To her left is an archway through which Brielle can see a sitting room. Exposed wood beams support a pitched ceiling. Sofas of varying sizes are arranged around a great stone fireplace, a round olive carpet at the foot of the hearth. Against one wall are a pair of loaded bookshelves, a grandfather clock, and two curio cabinets with streaked glass doors shielding an amalgam of collectibles. Opposite the cabinets is the bay window she'd seen from the outside, wider and taller than it had looked from the driveway. The panes of glass begin at her shins and stretch high enough that she couldn't reach the top of the frame even if she stretched her hands above her head.

Brielle shifts the duffel bag further up her shoulder. Turning on the spot, she faces the long hallway with several doors that, for the most part, are shut. One on the left at the far end, and three on the right. Opposite her, she can just make out the bottom of a circular stairwell.

To Brielle's right, double doors open into an office with a handsome cherry desk positioned in the center. Two asymmetrical clamshell armchairs upholstered in a faded floral fabric face the desk. She's struck by the odd juxtaposition between the apparent desire to furnish this place in the style of a grand mansion and the fact that the residence at the Garrick Estate can't be much more than two thousand square feet, if that—respectable, to be certain, but not overwhelming.

Turning back, she enters the living room, careful not to touch anything as she wanders over to the bay window. Standing in the alcove, she can see her car parked on the gravel drive. Beyond the shallow, grassy field is the wall of oak trees blocking the town from view even at this raised vantage point. She can't see the next house over, though she knows the neighbors aren't more than a couple hundred feet away.

A gust of wind kicks up outside and the house *grooooans* in response, urging Brielle to move on. Beside the cabinets, in the back corner of the sitting room, is another arched doorway. This one leads into a combination kitchen and dining area. Along the wall she spies a light switch and flicks it on. The room is immediately bathed in a yellow, incandescent glow, though the hanging light fixture is so thoroughly coated in cobwebs and dust that she can barely make out the design in the painted glass.

A long rectangular table sits before the doorway with chairs for ten. Beyond, the kitchen area is all faded ivory tiles and pine cabinets. Lemon wallpaper covers two of the walls, while the others are a mosaic of teal, white, and yellow geometric designs. The stars and a half-moon are visible through the skylight above. Brielle has never liked cooking much, but her mother had, and she can imagine how much this kitchen would've impressed her.

Another door leads back into the hallway.

Brielle stares at the front door on the other end of the corridor. Is it just her imagination, or is it disproportionately shrouded in shadow?

Behind her, the stairs spiral up into darkness. Frosted windows stretch the height of the room but provide little light.

Across the hallway from the kitchen, she enters a bedroom. The light switch snaps loudly when she flips it on, revealing a queen bed against the center of the back wall with a red comforter cascading over the sides like the lava flow of an erupting volcano. A mid-century dresser takes up another wall, clashing with most of the house's older decorative elements. Strangely enough, there's a leather hard-shell suitcase still resting on it—a remnant of the past.

Along the right-hand wall is a closed door, which Brielle reasons must lead to a bathroom, given that there is but one room left on the first floor, sandwiched between this room and the front office.

She tries the handle, but it's locked.

"Hello?" Brielle asks the silence again. She gets no response.

Thinking this as good a place as any to call her own for the night, Brielle sets down her duffel bag beside the suitcase. The house shifts again in the wind, a higher creak to fill the void. She follows the sound with her eyes as it runs the full length of the room from the curtained window to the locked door.

Brielle returns to her bag and feels around inside—an analog tape recorder, a film camera, some sensors, and her journal. There are a few candles and special oils too, but she rarely resorts to those. More often than not, spirits *want* to move on—they're naturally drawn to the great unknown—she just has to figure out what stands in their way.

But, of course, that requires *meeting* a spirit.

Unfolding the laptop, Brielle turns it on. If Nadine has been paying the electricity and water bills, perhaps she's introduced other amenities as well. The laptop boots quickly, but when she discovers that the house hasn't yet been wired for Internet, she puts it away again. No need for that anymore, which is unfortunate but not entirely surprising. There aren't enough haunted dwellings with Wi-Fi.

Instead, she takes out her journal and makes a quick sketch of the house from memory, as well as a diagram of the floorplan.

When she's finished, Brielle yawns. It can't be very late, but she did do an awful lot of driving today. On the bedside table sits an old alarm clock that must be from the eighties or early nineties. She's surprised it still works. For no other reason than peace of mind, she takes out her phone and uses it to correct the red digital readout. Shy of nine thirty and she's *this* tired? She must be getting old.

Another creak, only this time there is no howl of wind to accompany it.

Brielle stays very still, ear cocked toward the open door. Was that movement? She can't tell from in here.

Standing, she tiptoes as quietly as she can to the hall, her breath slow and measured. The thick silence has settled around her ears once more, daring her to be the one to break it. Her hand grips the doorframe as she leans her head out.

Brielle had forgotten to turn off the light in the kitchen, and so the warm glow spills out in a fan across the floor. Nothing seems to have moved within, the chairs still neatly arranged around the long table. The circular stairwell beside her remains dark and empty, the steps curling up and out of sight. And the hallway—

Something moves down at the other end, near the front door. Brielle sucks in a sharp breath. Could it have been a ghost? The movement was too quick—whatever it had been darting into the office.

"Hello?" Brielle calls, leaving the bedroom. Her footsteps replace the silence, a rhythmic thudding that quickens as she goes. Halfway along the corridor, she sees the office doors swing shut with a resounding slam that echoes through the house.

"I'm here to help you," Brielle says. She grabs one of the handles and twists, but it doesn't move. She pushes on the double doors, but they don't budge either. In fact, they've been locked so solidly that she wonders for a moment whether they'd actually been open before. Whether she's sure they're doors and not simply a wall with handles.

Brielle raps her knuckles against the wood. "Please, I mean you no harm."

She straightens as chimes follow next. The grandfather clock strikes the half hour.

Confused, Brielle turns on the spot to face the open archway into the living room. Can the clock be running after all these years? How is this possible? As she'd come to understand it, the house had been abandoned for decades, and yet the notes ring loud and unmistakable. She can see the pendulum swinging behind the glass. How had she missed that before?

As the note dies, every light goes with it.

Brielle's head swivels, gazing up and down the empty hallway. Whereas there'd been a glow emanating from the kitchen and the bedroom, now there is nothing but darkness. Pure, encroaching darkness.

A loud, elongated creak fills the air. Brielle raises her eyes toward the ceiling above. In the silence that has engulfed the Garrick house, the noise is deafening. It echoes through the structure as though emanating from every wall at once. Brielle has heard creaks like this before; she expects them—in fact, she's been waiting for one ever since she arrived. And now that it's here, she almost breathes a sigh of relief.

The noise ends abruptly, and is followed by a harsh thud as something strikes a wall. Brielle was right—it's coming from overhead.

Thud.

Keeping her eyes trained on the ceiling, she reaches for the hall light switch. But as her fingers find the plastic protrusion, she hesitates. Many spirits have an aversion to electricity—especially the emotionally charged ones. She doesn't want to chase the ghost away.

Brielle leaves the light off and drifts down the hallway toward the stairs. Toward where she believes the ghost will appear.

Thud.

The noise is so close to the stairwell that Brielle expects to see the spirit at any second. She holds her breath, heart racing and hands clenched, eyes straining against the dark. This is always the moment of greatest fear in any job—learning what she's up against. She makes certain her knees aren't locked; she stands tall, alert. Ready.

Nothing comes. The noises cease.

For twenty long seconds, Brielle doesn't move, prepared for the haunting to continue. The house sighs in the breeze, the normal groans commence, but the bangs are at an end. She relaxes her posture, her breath coming steadily again. While the anticipation subsides, her disappointment rises. She would rather know what was making the noise. But perhaps tonight will not be the night.

A high-pitched, throat-rending scream tears through the dark, straightening Brielle's spine and rippling her flesh. She spins on the spot, turning toward the cry, and takes off in a sprint down the hallway.

The scream continues, unwavering in pitch and volume. The unmistakable anguish of a soul in turmoil. She feels it in her gut as she nears the front door, coming into view of the living room.

Standing before the bay window is the decaying figure of a woman in a bloodied nightgown. Her hair is tangled, sizable chunks torn from her scalp. Her eyes are sunken, skin purple and sagging off her bones. Down her front spills an unceasing river of blood, further staining her tattered garment and pooling on the floor. She stares out the window screaming, but as Brielle comes into view, the woman ceases her agonized wail. They lock eyes and Brielle gets a good look at the bloodshot whites around her ringed pupils.

"Who—who are you?" Brielle says, fighting the rising urge to flee. She senses her feelings are being manipulated. The woman's spirit is highly driven by emotion, and without a corporeal form, that emotion radiates from her like mist.

Rivers of red course down her face. She stares Brielle down, but doesn't speak.

"Who are you?" Louder this time, more confidence. Quell the fear. Push it down. "I'm here to help you."

Brielle takes a step forward.

The woman opens her decaying mouth again, strings of blood flowing over her lips. But instead of an answer, she releases another devastating scream. It is all Brielle can do not to press her palms over her ears to muffle the cry. She grits her teeth against the inhuman wail, a wave of terror and desolation suddenly washing over her.

Then the woman disappears, and Brielle is left with the unobstructed view of the night beyond the window and the muffled sounds of a car driving in the distance.

CONCERNING COMPANY

When she awakens, the house is silent and still.

Brielle sits up, letting the top of her sleeping bag fall away. As a rule, she doesn't sleep in the beds of haunted dwellings. They're often sources of emotional turmoil for ghosts and therefore not something she wants her presence associated with. Not to mention sheets that have been left alone for as long as the ones in the Garrick house would be coated in years of dust and who knows what else. A residual morning frigidity clings to the air, and so she wraps herself in a coat before cautiously getting up to check the locked "other" door.

To her surprise, it opens easily. That timing is something to take note of—at some point in the day, entry into this room and the office ceases until morning.

Brielle goes in. She flicks a switch and an orange incandescent bulb powers to life, washing what is indeed a bathroom in a tinted glow. The floor and the counters are white tile, as are the walls to waist height. Above that, they're covered in a green wallpaper: cranes wading through marshland. A combination bathtub and shower stands against one wall, while a boxy toilet with a wooden seat sits in the corner. There are two doors to the bathroom; one leads to the bedroom she slept in, and the other out into the hall. She notices this second door is damaged, the side jamb cracked around the lock. Despite this, it had somehow remained impassable last night.

Brielle catches a glimpse of herself in the mirror, looking tired and haggard as though she's just slept on a hardwood floor. There are no signs of any spirits inside the bathroom, and so, grateful that someone is paying the bills, she decides to take a hot shower. Running back into her bedroom, she grabs the threadbare towel she keeps with her at all job visits, then sits for several minutes on the rim of the tub, her hand lingering beneath the flow as she waits for heat. When she begins to wonder whether the water heater works after all, the temperature rises.

Standing in the steam under a miracle of water pressure clears her senses. Brielle runs her fingers repeatedly through her hair, using the tips to massage her scalp. All the while, she has her eyes closed, envisioning the nightmarish spectacle from the night before.

The woman by the window.

Many ghosts manifest in gruesome ways—particularly those who have died under traumatic circumstances. The event becomes the thing which defines them. Obviously, this is the case for whoever the woman was—drenched in blood, decaying, visibly distressed. The trick will be finding what binds her here and how to resolve it.

Brielle shuts off the water and is shocked by how quickly the cold of the house settles into her skin.

After getting dressed, she checks her phone. She has three missed calls and one voicemail, all of them from her brother.

Leaning against the dresser, she sighs, knowing what his message will be about. For five long minutes the little red voicemail icon mocks her with its miniscule urgency, and she debates whether or not now is the time to return his call. Then her stomach breaks the silence with a wail of aggression, and she decides now is as good a time as any to do something.

Brielle grabs her coat, knowing if it's cold inside the house, it must be freezing outside. As she goes, she brings the phone to her ear and checks her pocket for the key. Now that sunlight pours through the windows, the house is not so morose. The rooms are quirky and charming rather than ominous and threatening. She can see the touches left by past owners—aging wallpaper, ornate sconces, and the surprisingly well-preserved wooden flooring. She will have to look more carefully when she returns.

The voicemail begins.

"Hey, Bri, it's Kam. I swung by your place, but you were gone, so I'm guessing you're out of state again. I'm not—"

Brielle hangs up before her brother's recording can finish. She dials his number, her fingers so practiced she barely has to think. In under five seconds, the phone is back to her ear, with muffled sounds of ringing on the other end.

He picks up on the third ring.

"So, you up and leave?"

"*Hi* to you too, Kam."

"I didn't think you'd be in the mood for greetings."

"I took a case, okay," Brielle says, trying to keep her voice level though she feels a flare of indignation that is—in all probability—rooted more in guilt than actual offense.

"Yeah, I'm sure it was really necessary on such short notice." Kam is obviously frustrated, looking for a fight maybe. His normally good-natured tone is nowhere to be found. Hearing him this way causes her guilt to ratchet up a notch. After all, it takes a lot to rattle him.

"Look, I needed a little space, okay. I'm—" She struggles to find the words. "I'm not as good at handling these sorts of things."

"Brielle." Incredulity sends his voice up an octave. "You literally spend your life around dead people."

"Yes, but they're already dead when I meet them."

"Does that make much of a difference?"

"They're also not Mom."

He sighs, a rush of static that blends into the wind around her. Brielle can imagine him on the other end of the call, kneading his temple with his fingers, eyes shut. It's what he does whenever he needs to calm himself. He's so good at that, recognizing when he needs a moment. Like most people, Brielle rarely recognizes she's riled up until it's too late—it gets her into trouble. Typically, it's why she does her best not to get anywhere near that level of emotion.

"I'm not mad," he says when his moment is through. "At least, I'm not mad at you for needing some space."

"Thank you."

"I do want to know though…"

"Yeah?"

"Will you be back for her funeral?"

Brielle looks out across the grounds of the Garrick Estate. At night, they seemed so much larger than they do beneath the gray sky. Perhaps it was the darkness that extended the field's reach. The unknown. She leans against a column at the edge of the stairs, wishing she could see some sign of the town through the foliage— maybe the glimmer of the ocean. Then at least she wouldn't have this growing sense of isolation inside her. Instead, she's left with the wall of trees.

"Bri?"

"Yeah, of course," she says, shaking herself out of a stupor. "Yes, I'll be there."

"Five days," he says.

"I know. The job shouldn't take too long."

He pauses again, maybe judging whether or not he believes her, though he wouldn't dare voice that concern.

"Alright," he says. "I'll see you in a few days then."

"Yeah," Brielle replies, then hangs up. She runs a hand over her face, her fingers cold from exposure. Five days. She should be able to make it in five days. Most jobs only take one or two—just a bit of poking around. And if that's not enough time? Well, then she could always leave and come back. There's no specified deadline, and attending her mother's funeral is pretty important. It's the final goodbye, after all—unless, of course, there's a ghost. But Mom's death, despite it being a prolonged battle, was relatively peaceful. She knew she was dying. She'd accepted her fate. There were no surprises. So there should be no reason for a ghost.

If she's being honest with herself, though, the prospect of her mother returning as a spirit is not the bit that gives Brielle pause. She imagines hordes of out-of-town relatives already descending— filling up Kamnan's house because they'd rather not pay for a hotel. Until the funeral, they'll gather nightly. Crowding into too tight of rooms with their loud voices. Singing their praises of Brielle's mother: how she was a perfect, beautiful angel who could do no wrong.

And if Brielle were home, she'd be subjected to that mess right now.

She shouldn't feel bad. Kamnan enjoys that sort of company. He hadn't called her because he was angered by her absence but because he wanted to make sure she'd be back for the funeral. And she would. Brielle had agreed to go.

She takes her car keys out of her pocket. Descending the steps, she decides it's time for something to eat. Her stomach is shouting at her. So she climbs into her vehicle and leaves the estate, driving that short but transportive distance to where the rest of the coastal town lies. Short, old buildings line the narrow lanes, people scattered along the sidewalks in winter clothing, and the pale Atlantic in the distance. She passes small wooden churches with pointed bell towers, parks coated in red blankets of fallen leaves.

After purposely wandering through the town, Brielle settles on a diner—crowded for a weekday—and snags herself a small booth. It's a little late for breakfast, so she orders lunch, wanting something substantial to tide her over. Meanwhile, the guilt never leaves her. As she waits for her food, she stares at the tabletop wondering if maybe taking the job at the Garrick Estate had been the wrong thing to do after all. It had felt so right in the moment— the perfect timing. Being contained to her hometown had built to a suffocating pressure, culminating in her mom's passing. She'd needed the space to clear her head, and the job was there. But at the very least, maybe she could've told Nadine to wait until after the funeral. Nobody had pushed her to start right away.

"Your burger, darling," the waitress says, setting down a plate. "You need anything else, hon?"

"I'm great, thanks," Brielle replies with a smile. She almost asks the waitress to stay, longing for someone else to talk to, but she doesn't. The waitress has work to do, and she doesn't owe Brielle anything beyond the delivery of her meal.

Watching the woman go, a sudden urge comes over Brielle. She takes out her phone and dials.

"Bri?" asks the voice on the other end. "It's been so long!"

Brielle runs a shameful hand through her hair, knowing that the absence is her fault. "Vivian! I know! Far too long."

She's grateful that there's no sign of discontent in her friend's voice—not that she should expect any. Their last rendezvous hadn't ended with animosity; rather, Brielle had simply let the distance grow. But she figures both of them are adult enough to understand that life happens. And weeks turn into months without calls. Sometimes even years.

"What's going on, girl?"

Brielle laughs nervously. "I'm so sorry, Viv. Time got away from me. I've been meaning to call, but—anyway. I'm working a case in your neck of the woods and I was hoping we could get coffee while I'm here."

"What!" Vivian sounds so excited, Brielle feels another rush of guilt. She really shouldn't have gone so long without communicating. "Most definitely. How long are you going to be around?"

"Oh, you know how these things go. I can't really tell."

"I'm free tomorrow."

Brielle smiles. Vivian has always made time for her.

"Yeah, tomorrow sounds great."

"Where exactly are you?"

"Camden."

"Really close, then! Yeah, uh…" She pauses, and Brielle can hear rustling through the telephone. "If you don't mind driving up to Belfast, I know a kick-ass place for paninis. We can get coffee first and then have lunch after."

"Sounds great," Brielle says, knowing that she probably shouldn't spend too much time off the case but willing to let her focus waver. A part of her wonders why she feels so compelled to go out of her way to visit Vivian. Normally, she's laser focused until the job is done. "How about ten?"

"Make it ten thirty and I'll be there."

Brielle laughs, marveling at how some things never change. They say their goodbyes and hang up, leaving Brielle in a fog of excited anticipation. She hasn't felt this ready to meet a friend in some time, and the excitement is almost enough to make her wonder why she doesn't do it more often.

Brielle finishes her meal in silence, then returns to her car and drives back to the Garrick house, eager to resume her investigation. Last night's introduction had certainly piqued her interest, especially after the appearance of the terrifying woman. But much of the house remains unexplored. Now, in the light of day, she can assess the finer details and get a better feel for what spiritual turmoil grips the property.

After she drags the gate closed behind her, Brielle returns to her locked car in the circular driveway, panting just a bit more than she'd like to admit. Then she mentally gathers herself, doing her best to clear her mind of all the morning's debris.

Begin.

The Garrick house is centered amid several acres of land—most of which is dying grass and monstrous weeds—and separated from the outside world by four solid walls of burly oak trees. Sagging stairs lead up to a weathered porch with vine-like filigree hanging down from the awning. The wide front door would not look out of place in a gothic church—heavy and solid with a prominent iron handle and two green stained-glass cutouts. Most of the windows

are old leaded glass, cut into diamond panes by black iron. The large
bay window to the left of the front door is the sole exception, in
that each of the three segments is a single rectangular sheet from
top to bottom.

From there, Brielle begins her trek around the side of the
house, sticking to the path of garden stones, which, though also
overgrown, is the most navigable route. There isn't much to be said
for the grounds. Most of it is unused field, save for a small garden
in the back. The flowerbeds burst with weeds and the wooden trellis
reaching up to a second-story window is broken in several places
and covered in dead ivy, but she imagines at some point, the area
could've been charming.

Elsewhere, the house is a continuous collection of jarring
features: mustard yellow where it's shingle siding, mauve where it's
scalloped. The trim is olive in some areas and pastel blue in others.
Brielle can't imagine that the color combination ever worked when
the paint was fresh, but now that it's spent decades fading and
peeling, it's surprisingly palatable and maybe even appealing in a
quirky way. There's faded gilding, the odd weather vane, and vines
reaching their spindly fingers toward the rooftop.

After circling the outside, she finds herself at the foot of the
front steps. Each one *creeeeeaks* on her way up to the door. Brielle
draws the key out of her pocket. It's massive compared to the rest
of the keys she owns. Wide, gaudily toothed, and brass. And despite
the age, the lock gives her no troubles.

She pushes the door open, letting herself back inside.

Light from the overcast sky streams through the windows,
giving Brielle an odd sensation of both comfort and tension. There's
a wealth of built-up energy in this place waiting to be released. She
can feel it in the silence, pushing up on the underside of the

floorboards, running through the pipes, hanging from the light fixtures. It's there, just beyond her field of vision if only she focuses her mind just a bit more.

"May I help you?" says a voice from behind her.

Brielle spins around, heart in her throat.

INN SPIRITS

Behind Brielle stands a worn-looking woman. Not the terrifying spirit dressed in tatters and dripping blood, but someone who has, nevertheless, seen her fair share of the world's darker facets.

Brielle places a hand over her heart, feeling the pounding beats against the inside of her ribcage.

"Sorry," she says. "I didn't hear anyone coming."

The woman smiles blankly. "That happens sometimes."

And this causes Brielle's eyebrows to ascend her forehead. "Are you…?"

"Dead? I'm afraid so."

Brielle takes in the woman's entire appearance. She's dressed like someone who's very comfortable being comfortable—a low-cut black T-shirt over acid-wash jeans and wrinkled boots. Her matted gray hair has been pulled into an unsuccessful updo from which more strands have escaped their trappings than remain in place. Her face is pale but blotchy, with sagging eyelids, and her smile reveals crooked teeth as gray as the overcast Atlantic.

She could be anywhere from sixty to a hundred years old.

"I'm Brielle Panya."

"Panya." She lets the name sit on her tongue. "Haven't heard that one before."

"It's Thai."

"I see." The ghost woman nods politely. "Call me Rizette."

Brielle cannot hide her confusion. She's still in awe.

"Are you always so…vibrant?" she asks, tempted to circle the woman in order to take in every crisp detail. She knows from experience, however, that this might make Rizette uncomfortable. And spirits who are uncomfortable often leave.

"I'm guessing you aren't dead then?" Rizette asks.

Brielle shakes her head. "No, I can't say that I am."

"Well then, we haven't had one of you come along in quite some time."

Brielle has encountered two types of ghosts in her travels. One is almost like a cloud—changing shape and size, often at will. They appear in their corporeal states very seldom—and only then for a few seconds at a time—preferring to cause chaos as they embody the tumultuous emotions under which they died. They fly through walls and doors and cause surges in energy, resulting in terrifying experiences for the living who surround them. She would classify the woman from last night as this first kind.

The second type is calmer, almost always in the form of a human, and to some degree, solid. They can't pass through walls, but neither can they touch living matter like humans or plants. While Rizette seems like the second type of spirit, Brielle is still amazed. She's never met one who readily acknowledged they were a ghost. Normally, part of the process of setting them free is getting them to realize they've died. That knowledge, that admittance, is half the battle. Rizette seems to be not only cognizant of her state but comfortable with it.

"Shall I show you around then?" Rizette asks, as if giving a guided tour of the haunted house is part of her occupation.

Caught slightly off guard by this show of hospitality, Brielle takes a moment to collect herself. "I gave myself a partial tour last night—of the first floor, at least—but I didn't realize anyone else was here."

"Was it late in the evening?"

"Pretty late, yeah."

Rizette smiles.

"This is the living room," she says, diving headlong into her tour despite the implication that Brielle has already seen this area. She gestures as if she were a realtor modeling a home. "All the floors are original to the 1893 construction of the Garrick home, but as you can see, they've been kept in great condition. The hearth is also original, as is the chair rail. However, I've been told the bay window was a later addition after the Garrick family had sold it off."

"I'm sorry," Brielle says, interrupting Rizette's recounting of the house's history. "Who are you—or rather, who were you in relation to this place?"

"Oh, right, I thought maybe you'd know already." Rizette runs a hand across the back of one of the sofas. Brielle notices that very little dust is displaced by her touch. "I was the last owner of the estate," she says. "I'm the one who ran it as a bed and breakfast until the early 1990s."

"And you bought it to make an inn?"

"No, no." She shakes her head adamantly. "I lived here for many years before that."

"Did—"

"We can continue across the hall into the office."

"Yes, but—"

Her guide leaves the room, and Brielle has no choice but to follow. In the office, Rizette walks around to the opposite side of the desk.

"This is where I received folks," she says. "I still keep the guest book out just for old times' sake."

She points down at a leatherbound journal lying on the surface. A merlot-colored ribbon hangs out the bottom of the pages somewhere past the middle.

Now that she's in the office, Brielle can see maps hanging on the wall behind the desk. They seem to all be hand drawn—inked schematics of large cities. San Francisco. Manhattan Island. London. Half obscured by a bookshelf in the back corner of the room is the door of a closet. A glass light ornamented with embossed leaves hangs from the ceiling.

"I was hoping to fill all the pages," Rizette says, then chuckles conspiratorially. "But I suppose that isn't likely now."

"Stranger things have happened," says Brielle.

"Have they?"

"I've seen some contenders."

Rizette observes her, perhaps wondering what Brielle means by this. There's the obvious question, which she hasn't sought to ask. And Brielle wonders if she's going to or if perhaps she doesn't want to know the answer.

"If you'll follow me," Rizette says, walking around Brielle and out of the office again. Torn, Brielle follows her.

She has half a mind to insist Rizette cease the tour. If she's going to be shown the first-floor rooms, she'd rather it be at her own, more in-depth pace. But a ghostly tour guide is a luxury she's not often privy to. So even if Rizette is determined to charge through the Garrick house at breakneck speed, Brielle feels compelled to play along, waiting for the important tidbits Rizette might naturally let slip.

As soon as they enter the hallway, the bathroom door opens. Out walks a thin man with close-cropped dark hair and pale blue eyes. He wears baggy clothes, emphasizing his slight frame. The newcomer spots them with a nervous glance.

"Parrish Creed, I was wondering when you might join us," Rizette says.

"I heard you," he says. His voice is high and nasally. "I knew you'd get to me eventually, so I didn't come running."

"Are you also…a spirit?" Brielle asks, looking back and forth between Rizette and Parrish. How many ghosts are in this house?

He nods sullenly.

"I'm Brielle."

"Pleased to make your acquaintance." Even though the words are welcoming, he says them in such a way that all meaning is lost. Brielle might've taken offense to his welcome, but she's used to ghosts being a heightened version of their living counterparts. After all, the only things that are left of them are emotions and memories. "I hear you're not one of us."

Another self-aware spirit.

"No, I'm not," Brielle confirms.

"Are you here to vanish us, then?"

"I prefer to think of it as helping you find peace." She hopes her smile is comforting. "But I suppose you're not incorrect. Yes, that's why I'm here."

"Thank God," Parrish mutters. He turns on his heel and strides back into the bathroom.

"That's the downstairs restroom," Rizette says.

"You'll be the only one using it." Parrish's voice carries with a slight echo. "Good thing the bills are being paid again or you wouldn't have any water."

They follow him, using the second interior door to reach the bedroom where Brielle slept. Her duffel bag is still perched on the dresser, an assortment of items strewn across the bed where she'd left them.

"This is the first guestroom," Rizette says.

"*My* guestroom," Parrish says.

"Yours?" Brielle asks.

Parrish nods.

"That must be your suitcase, then. I'm guessing you died here?"

"Oh no," Rizette says, stepping around in front of Brielle. "Rather, that's not at all a certainty. Parrish and I—we don't have any recollection of our deaths. Not where. Not when. Not how. It's just…gone."

"But you know who you were and that you're dead. You must have some recollection?"

"It gets hazy, the closer you get to the—uh, *event*," Parrish says, stumbling over the last word. "I could tell you all about my childhood if you wanted to know, but I couldn't tell you anything about my stay here. Except that this was my room. That I know as well as my name."

Brielle raises an eyebrow, but rather than making a comment, she takes a mental note. Ghosts not remembering their own death is not uncommon—again, that's part of the letting go bit—but usually that's *why* they don't know they're dead. These are certainly some strange specters. Though, if she's being honest, she's a bit happy that they're fully "functional," if that makes any sense. The toughest part of any job is trying to figure out who the players are and what their motivations were. With these two, she can easily have a conversation and hopefully get to the root of what makes them tick.

"Are you *staying*?" Rizette says, noticing Brielle's bag.

Brielle looks down at her belongings, wondering if she should've kept them in a neater pile instead of strewn haphazardly. "Yeah, when I'm working a haunting, I generally stay on-site. It gives me the most time to figure out what's happening."

"Surely you'd want to stay somewhere more pleasant?"

"It's fine. I've spent a million nights in haunted houses."

Brielle has handled more than two hundred jobs in her decade of service. More than half of them were houses, and for most she stayed on-site. It's easier that way, especially given the fact that most angry spirits prefer the dark—clichéd as that might be.

"I don't think we've ever had anyone living here before," Rizette says. "Well, after I died, of course."

"There's a first time for everything." Brielle smiles.

"You might regret that decision after a few nights," Parrish says. So they *do* know about the other woman.

"The more I know, the easier it'll be to fix your situation."

"If you insist," Rizette says. "I can move Parrish's—"

"It's alright to leave it—"

They reach for the hard-shell suitcase simultaneously. Rizette grabs the handle first, and in the next second, Brielle's hand passes through hers to curl around the same spot. The effect is sudden, cold, and clammy. Brielle has had this happen a number of times, but even so it's always surprising—as if her living body is adamantly against getting used to the sensation. She withdraws her hand with the same intensity of someone who has just touched a hot stove, shaking out her icy fingers.

"I'm so sorry," Rizette says, gasping.

"It's alright," Brielle assures her. "Stable ghosts are always a lot more shocking to the touch. Probably because you're so much closer to a physical state."

"Stable ghosts?"

"Sorry, as opposed to fleeting ghosts—they're my own terms. Stable ghosts are the ones who are solid when interacting with non-living matter. At least, while visible. Fleeting ghosts appear infrequently and don't have many spatial limitations."

"Huh," Rizette says, nodding with an inquisitive look. "I see."

After recovering from the shock, they leave through the bedroom's other exit, back into the long hallway.

"Last is the kitchen," Rizette says, leading the way. The kitchen looks much the same as it did the night before, only brighter and more cheerful. "The tile work's all mine, thank you very much. Took me damn near two years to get done, and now I have the pleasure of seeing it every single day."

"Lucky for us," Parrish says, then turns to Brielle. "That concludes our tour. Dinner is served at seven."

Brielle smiles politely. Ghost don't eat.

"But there's another floor," she says. "Why are we stopping here?"

"It's best not to go up there," Rizette says.

Brielle raises an eyebrow. If that's the case, then she knows exactly where she intends to go next.

"Why not?" she asks, wondering if they'll be willing to respond.

Rizette doesn't look like she wants to answer. So Brielle turns to Parrish, who has his feet up on what looks like a very expensive dining table.

"On account of the bad energy," he says, his tone disinterested. "We can feel it emanating all the time. It's like a fire: the closer we get to it, the hotter it is. Only it's not heat, if you get my meaning."

"It's bad energy," Brielle finishes.

"Only Laurel can stand it up there, but that's because it's his *place*." Rizette looks almost embarrassed to admit this. She averts her gaze, lips pursed.

"Laurel?" Brielle asks.

"Yeah, he lives upstairs."

"And he doesn't feel the bad energy?"

"He does, but he tolerates it better than we do," Parrish says.

"And he's not the source of the bad energy, right?"

"Oh no, definitely not," Rizette says, shaking her head. Brielle turns to Parrish, seeking for the man to corroborate the innkeeper's story. He shakes his head as well, but doesn't make eye contact.

"Well, I'll need to meet Laurel then," Brielle states. "Does he come down?"

"Sometimes," Rizette says. Her voice gains a husky growl when it lowers, likely the result of years of heavy smoking. She raises her eyes to the ceiling and Brielle does the same. "Mostly he keeps to himself up there. Like I said, it's his place."

The house creaks under the influence of a strong wind—nails groaning as the wood shifts.

"Thank you for the tour," Brielle says absentmindedly.

"Are you going up there?"

"I'll have to if you want my help," she says.

"We'll be here when you get back," Parrish says, getting up and slumping through the doorway into the sitting room. He must've been a joy in life.

Brielle tears her eyes away from the ceiling. The innkeeper has become entranced, staring upward unblinking. That she doesn't breathe makes her look even more like a statue. Her stillness is unsettling. Brielle leaves her in the kitchen.

She journeys into the unknown portion of the house, beginning with the stairwell. Tall amber-glass windows stretch the difference between the first and second floors, casting calming light into the circular space. Again, she is reminded of the marked difference between the Garricks' grand vision for the home and its modest size. So far, each room has been decorated with elaborate crown molding of the richest brown hues. Cherry, or maybe mahogany—she's never had a discerning eye for types of wood. Matching wainscoting in the dining area. Filigree around some of the doors. The railing that leads up the interior of the curved staircase is of a similar ornate styling. Above the stairwell hangs a glass chandelier. It's not that any of the details are cheap or out of place, it's that their grandiosity is muted by tighter spaces. And maybe that was a necessary tradeoff: a small size to retain the touches which make a grander residence feel opulent. It's far more character than any dwelling she's ever called home.

Brielle reaches the second-floor landing, met by a long corridor that is a dark mirror of the one below. This hallway seems much barer. There is still the glass sconce on the wall, along with the wallpaper and chair rail. But there are no paintings or photographs or wall art of any kind. And the window at the other end has been covered with sheer curtains heavy enough that they diffuse the light past utility. They provide more of a glow than true illumination.

She flips the light switch with a heavy click, and the bulb that comes to life behind the sconce is weak. There are only three doors on this level, all along the left-hand wall. These, Brielle reasons, must be two guest rooms and a bathroom.

Does the second floor emanate a far more dreadful atmosphere? Or is the sense inside her merely the power of suggestion? Both Rizette and Parrish had expressed their unwillingness to come up here.

Brielle approaches the first door and knocks firmly but politely. With her ear inclined, she listens for sounds from inside, but none are audible.

"Laurel?" she asks, then grabs the handle. The door is locked. She tries a little harder, but the barrier is steadfast. "Laurel?"

When she receives no reply, she moves on to the other doors.

The second leads to a bathroom much like the one below: a bathtub against one corner, a pedestal sink, a small frosted-glass window set high in the far wall. As she'd assumed, the last door leads to a final bedroom. In this one, two of the walls are covered floor to ceiling with bookshelves. Every bit of shelf space is occupied by monochromatic spines in deep colors, their titles embossed in serifed gold lettering. It's mostly old novels and reference materials, nothing that she finds particularly noteworthy. While she recognizes a few of the novelists, none of the present tomes are the classics they're known for. The farther she looks, she wonders if this is somewhat by design—an anti–greatest hits collection. She finds herself at the window, peering down beneath the overcast sky at her car. No ghosts here.

Glad to have seen (almost) the entire house, Brielle heads back the way she came, the solitary thud of her footsteps following her out of the bedroom. She's just about to enter the landing at the top of the stairs when she notices a staff of some sort hanging in the corner. She'd missed it when entering the corridor, but now that she's headed the other way, it's visible.

The staff is tall—almost six feet, she would guess—made of dark, smooth wood. There are few embellishments besides the floral crown around the bottom end. The other side, however, is capped with a small metal hook. This hook is how the staff is stored in the corner—hung on a jutting nail—but Brielle imagines it must be for something else. She looks down the hall again and wonders if maybe it's for opening high windows. She has seen rods for that sort of thing. But none of these windows appear high enough to warrant this tool.

Replacing it on the nail, Brielle moves to the stairwell, peering over the banister at the tiles below. Their red-brown hue reminds her faintly of drying blood. Her thoughts are always so morbid when she's on a job.

And then she hears a door behind her open. It's the room that was locked.

Laurel steps out.

He's built like a redwood tree: tall and wide and sturdy as all hell. He's a fit man who looks to be in his late fifties with graying hair and worn olive skin. His eyes are as darkly green as a nameless pond in a backwoods. They search Brielle with a wary intensity.

"Who are you?" he asks.

"My name is Brielle," she says. "I'm here to help you all move on."

He raises an eyebrow, apparently interested. "Is that so?"

He stares at her hard, churning through an amalgam of thoughts she can't guess at. If he's as happy about her motivations as the other two spirits, then this will be a very odd job indeed. She's never had the voluntary aid of her subjects—especially since most don't realize what she's doing, given their state of denial.

Laurel takes one step closer to her. "Then I will gladly help you in any way I can."

"Actually, I came up here looking for you."

"Me?" He chuckles. "Well, fancy that."

"I was hoping to ask you some questions, if you wouldn't mind."

"Questions?"

"About your life—what you remember, what you can tell me about your time here. Anything that might be helpful."

"I see." His expression becomes very serious. "Well, I'd certainly be happy to help in any way that I can. Should—"

"Can we talk in your room?" Brielle doesn't wait for an answer. She slips past him and enters the bedroom, eager to see the last unexplored corner of the house. Her heart hammers with anticipation.

This could be the answer.

But her excitement is unwarranted.

The guestroom where his spirit dwells is not unlike the others—floral wallpaper, a thick rug beneath a queen bed. Like her own, there's a dresser set against one wall with a mirror perched on top. The stale air is a mixture of dust, decay, and something pungent like ammonia. Perhaps the most noticeable difference is that while the window in her bedroom is covered by thick curtains, Laurel's has no covering at all. Instead, there's an unobstructed view of the dilapidated garden out back.

Brielle can't deny her disappointment. She'd been hoping for one of those moments where she immediately feels a surge of spiritual turmoil—a surefire sign that she's close to something important. Besides the general uneasiness of the second floor, Laurel's room doesn't feel any different from the rest of the house.

"I'd offer you a chair," Laurel says, "but I'm afraid I haven't got one."

"It's okay, I'm fine standing."

"As you wish."

"Could you begin by telling me what you remember about yourself?"

Laurel doesn't answer immediately. He frowns, turning away, and brings the fingertips of his right hand to his chin. She gives him the time he needs to recollect himself, not wanting to discourage his participation.

"About myself?" he says, wandering to the window. He stares down through the leaded glass, the view of the grounds outside warped by weather and time. From up here, it's easier to see just how tall and unkempt the field is. Knowing he can't leave, Brielle wonders if the image is comforting to the man or torturous. She can't decide which she would feel in his place. "I had a family. A wife whom I would do anything for and our precious daughter. We were happy together. Whole. That much, I'll never forget.

"My wife and I never fought—it sounds impossible, but I assure you it's true. We met our first year of college at a trivia night. It was the type of thing we liked to do. Dorky, I know, but we fell in love then and there, and it was clear right away that we would spend our lives together. It all fell into place—graduating side by side, marriage, buying a home, starting our family. Sometimes I used to sit back and wonder what I'd done to deserve so much perfection. And I knew it was my duty to make sure she felt the same way.

"I did everything I could for her. Loved every bit of her. It was easy to do. She was the most charming and beautiful woman I've ever met. Of course, when that's the case, you're never the only one who feels that way. Everyone found her charming and beautiful. *Everyone.* Even though she had the ring, there were still those who'd come flirting. Passing her incessant compliments even when she denied them attention. Those who'd try to do more than flirt. Those who tried to steal her affection."

Brielle understood. She could easily conjure the image of someone who fit these descriptions. She'd encountered a few of them herself. Men whose egos were too big to carry on their own—who needed to feel desired. Men whose affectionate advances could turn sour in an instant.

"There was one admirer who refused to relent. A woman, actually, who cooked at a restaurant we frequented. We complimented her food once, and that was all it took. This lady started running into my wife everywhere—the park, the grocery store, sometimes on her evening walks. At first, my wife thought she could handle the woman without me, but it got to the point that she had to get me involved. Whenever I confronted her, she only got more aggressive, telling me that I was only in her way. *I* was the problem.

"We found out that the restaurant fired her, probably because her behavior was so erratic. Dealing with her became a constant issue, to the point that I was afraid to answer the phone because I was so worried it would be her calling for my wife. She threatened me and my daughter—"

Laurel stops abruptly, his head hung, staring at the floor between his feet. Something in the memory has become too difficult for him—perhaps recalling his daughter. Or if not her, then the fear he'd felt trying to protect her.

"Things came to a head one night when we received a desperate letter from the woman detailing what amounted to a plot to kidnap my wife. We could've involved the police, but I didn't trust them to take the situation seriously enough. This woman was out of her mind. Delusional and obsessed." He turns his back to the window and rests against the frame. "I apologize, this is where the details start to get hazy."

"Please, take your time," Brielle says, though she hopes the details come back to him the more he concentrates. "Most spirits lose memories the closer they get to their deaths."

He nods, frowning, and when he speaks again it's slower than before. "We decided we had no choice but to leave. She knew where we lived. So long as that was the case, she wouldn't stop harassing us. We left our daughter with my parents and skipped town, figuring once we picked a place, we'd go back for her."

Laurel clasps his hands behind his back. Frustrated, he paces the length of the room a few times, all the while shaking his head and frowning. Brielle can see how much the lapse in memory disturbs him. This factual, straight-laced man is uncomfortable when failed by his own mind. It's the part of himself that he's always been accustomed to trusting. Without his memories, without his personal evidence, what does he have?

"I think we arrived here the first night—well, obviously we must have. But I think her stalker somehow followed us." He stops and sinks down onto the mattress to the grunt of the springs. "I can't remember anything after that. So I would have to assume that she killed us."

He looks up at Brielle with round green eyes.

"I think so," she says gently. "Your friends downstairs—"

He smiles when she says "friends."

"—are reluctant to come up to the second floor because they say it fills them with dread. The atmosphere is overbearing. Do you feel that?"

He nods.

"All the time, but in here"—Laurel scans the room with his eyes—"it goes away."

"Is this where you always regain consciousness?"

He nods again.

"Can you tell me something, Laurel?"

"Yes?"

"What was your wife's name?"

He closes his eyes. His chest expands as he breathes in deeply, though there will be no air to grace his lungs. "Salma."

Brielle feels a release of tension in her chest. "May I ask you something else?"

"By all means."

"Is your wife the woman in the window?"

And he nods a third time.

LOCKED DOORS

Darkness has descended upon the Garrick house by the time Laurel finishes his story. At the end of it, he becomes obstinate, staring into space as though he no longer knows Brielle is there. She decides to leave him to his thoughts, and as soon as the bedroom door gently closes of its own accord behind her, she *knows* it's locked.

Just to check her suspicions, she tries the handle. It doesn't move.

As she descends the stairs, Brielle's hunger catches up with her. She hasn't eaten since lunch, and hadn't thought to bring anything back for dinner. But she's too invested now to venture out again, wanting to keep her momentum going—to continue to uncover the lives of the many spirits who reside here. Instead, she vows that tomorrow she'll go to the grocery store in town. She has a feeling this job will last at least a few more days, and she'd rather not eat out for every meal.

Absentmindedly, she wanders into the kitchen to check her food storage options. The refrigerator is positively ancient, but it hums away in its shadowy corner.

"I've forgotten your name," says a voice from behind her. It's Parrish, leaning against the doorframe. His eyes are sunken and sallow. They must've been that way earlier and she hadn't noticed. He doesn't look well.

"Brielle," she reminds him.

"Right. Forgive my memory," he says, though he doesn't sound at all regretful. "Being dead and all that."

"I understand," Brielle reassures him.

"I'm tired of it," he says, looking her in the eyes. "I'm tired of the endless days. Always half aware. Blurring. I want them to end."

"I'm going to set you free," Brielle says.

"You seem like the type who gets things done." Somehow the statement almost sounds like an accusation. "You never stop."

She's not sure she likes Parrish. His demeanor is abrasive, and so far she can't tell whether he wants her help or is mocking her. She knows he's only a shadow of his living self, but she doubts whether she would've liked him more alive.

But it's not her job to like the people she's trying to save.

"I try my best," she says.

"I'm sure you'll have us out of here by tomorrow."

A twinge of guilt. "Maybe not tomorrow," she says, not wanting to lie. "But the day after I'm—"

"Why not tomorrow?" he asks, frowning.

Brielle regrets the conversation. "I'm just going to visit an old friend. No more than a couple hours, though. I'll be back by the afternoon."

"Isn't that nice." He smiles and reaches for his mouth as if used to grabbing at a cigarette. In the absence of one, his fingers slide over his chapped lips. "Only one night and you're already scrambling to get away. Of course, I don't blame you. I'd do the same if I could, but I've lost count of days."

"I'm not scrambling to get away," she says, shaking her head. "I'm just rarely in the area. I—She's a close friend."

"I hope she enjoys the visit. Bring her by, if you want."

"Who's there?" Rizette comes into view behind him.

Parrish sneers. "It's the living lady."

"Oh yes, uh—Brielle." Rizette smiles, proud of herself for remembering.

"Whatever." Parrish rolls his eyes and makes to leave.

"Wait," Brielle says. "Before you go, I was hoping to discuss what happened last night."

The sallow man halts and turns back to face her. "What *about* what happened last night?"

"Well, for starters, none of you were here."

"Our consciousness comes and goes," he says, one eyebrow raised. "Our time ends and we're done for the day. Almost like going to sleep every night."

"Your 'time'?" Brielle asks, and they nod. "Do you go somewhere else?"

"No," Rizette says. "We just sort of blink and the next moment it's morning again."

"Why?"

Rizette shrugs. "Don't know, that's just the way it's always been."

"I used to find it disconcerting," Parrish says. "Now I just think, 'Another fucking day.'"

"Is that why Laurel's door locked after I left?" Brielle asks. "His time is up?"

"Bingo."

"Does it have to do with the screaming woman by the window?"

The ghosts exchange glances.

"We're not sure," Rizette says. "We've hardly met her, seeing as she usually appears only after we're done for the day."

"Her presence is frightening," Brielle says.

"That's one way of putting it," Parrish says.

"Was she one of your guests?"

"I couldn't tell you," Rizette says, shaking her head. "The closer it gets to our own deaths, the less details we can recall. I can tell you—"

"Who you were, but little more," Brielle finishes. The minds of ghosts are maddeningly restricted. So much is predicated on emotion and not actual memory—though if she pries enough, she can sometimes get them to *accidentally* recall details while painting a larger picture. It works best when they're alone.

"Since you're here," Brielle says, "may I talk to you in private?"

"Talk to me?" Rizette crosses her arms over her chest. She looks to Parrish, who has no visible reaction whatsoever. Brielle wants to assure him that his own interview will follow, but the innkeeper continues. "I don't know how I can help. I don't really remember the woman."

"She's not the only thing I want to know about," Brielle says.

"If we met before her death, I have no memory of it," Rizette continues. "Like I said, I don't even remember when I died, so I'm not sure I can be of much help to you."

"It's alright," Brielle assures her. "I'll just ask you about the things you do remember. You never know what'll end up being important."

The innkeeper's stare is blank—she's obviously anxious about being interviewed. Earlier, she'd seemed excited about the prospect of Brielle attempting to free their spirits. But maybe she'd hoped to be minimally involved in that process.

What is she afraid of?

"Alright," Rizette says softly, barely above a whisper.

"Maybe if we went somewhere else? Your office, perhaps?"

The suggestion is met by stiff movements as Rizette disappears into the hallway. Parrish steps aside to let Brielle follow her, and together they walk to the office. Once inside, Brielle closes the doors behind her. Rizette sinks into the leather armchair behind her desk. It moves slightly to accommodate her presence—not so much as it would have were it bearing the weight of her living body, but enough to know she's there. She laughs nervously, a pained smile on her face.

"You know, people are so scared of haunted houses, but they really shouldn't be. Especially not this one," she says.

"What do you mean?" Brielle asks.

"I mean, if anyone'd taken the time to look around this place, they could've found all sorts of goodies. You can have them if you want, I don't mind."

Brielle frowns. "I—I don't think I could do that," she says. "I don't like to take from the places I work."

"Oh, come on." Rizette waves a hand. "All the trinkets in the living room are antiques, the cookware is real copper, and I'll have you know that my husband never trusted the banks so all our earnings are in a safe in the basement."

Taken aback, Brielle cocks her head. "Really?"

"Of course, of course." She laughs nervously again. "But everyone steers clear of the Garrick house."

Brielle is sorely tempted to take a look, though she's wary of believing the innkeeper. It's not that she thinks Rizette is lying, just that she might not know exactly what happened to her belongings after her death. A little bonus couldn't hurt though.

But now is not the time, and she needs Rizette to relax.

"Thank you for the generosity," she says. "But why don't you tell me about yourself?"

"Oh, right. Yes." Rizette stares down at her hands folded on the desk. She's silent and still, eyes unblinking until Brielle is seconds away from asking if something's the matter. She's barely begun her questioning. Surely she hasn't said anything out of line yet? But as soon as she opens her mouth, the woman's raspy voice breaks the silence. "I met my husband after the war ended. Surprised the hell out of my parents. They never thought I was ever going to settle down. For godsakes, I was only twenty-three, but I ran with the wrong crowds, they used to say—anyway, that's all in the past. And Barney was great, mind. One of those quiet types. A man of few words, but boy could he dance.

"I was entertaining at the Club Raven then, a classy place like you couldn't find nowadays. Five nights a week I was up on the stage, playing Ella and Billie. Andrew Pounds ran the Raven at the time, and he loved me because I could play for myself, see. He didn't have to hire musicians for my act—I did both. Should've paid me for both, but I was just happy to have the steady gig. A month after they said we'd won, Barney walked through that door. I could see in his eyes that he loved me from the moment we met, but I could also see he was haunted. He was a man who never stopped thinking about how bad things could get. Things he knew from experience.

"I wished he would've proposed to me then and there. That night I dedicated every song to him, but Barney took things slow—everything, and I mean that. Had to do things proper, like. So we didn't marry until nearly five years later, which was a shocker for some. Myself included. Many saw us as an odd couple. In those days, most people didn't wait that long before getting married, especially not when our thirties were getting so close. How fortunate that neither of us ever rushed to settle down with the wrong person."

"So, you were born in the 1920s?" Brielle asks. She assumes that by "the war," Rizette means World War II.

"Yes, ma'am," the innkeeper says. "1922, to be exact...Oh, it sounds so old saying it aloud. I'm afraid to ask what year it is now."

Brielle decides that's a rhetorical statement.

"Sorry for the interruption."

"No bother. It's why we're here, right? So you can ask questions." Rizette clears her throat, taking a moment to reorient herself in the story. "Yeah, I'm sure my parents had given up on me. By the time we said our vows, the whole ordeal was an enormous relief. I was the last of their children to be married off."

"Did you have many siblings?"

"Two older sisters. But they'd found spouses and were out of the house by twenty. My parents were already knee deep in grandchildren by the time Barney and I tied the knot."

Brielle smiles. Personally, she's never attempted to have children, though she is very fond of them. "Did you ever have kids of your own?"

At this, Rizette lets out a deep sigh that deflates her presence.

"No, unfortunately. Both of us would've loved to, but it was never in the cards. I tell myself that it was because we found each other too late. I wasn't so old, but people were always going on about my biological clock, not realizing that we were trying. I blamed myself. We lost pregnancy after pregnancy, and in the end decided the hurt outweighed our desire to keep trying.

"Like I said before, Barney was a quiet, haunted man. And each time I miscarried, I could see his ghosts multiplying. We bought this house so we could have our family, but the home was never filled. The empty rooms remained a dark reminder of what we never had. Thinking about it later, I believe that fact played more of a role in Barney's decline than I originally gave it credit for. If we'd have moved…"

She freezes, chin resting on the tops of her folded hands, elbows on the desk as if she's praying. The overhead light illuminates her from above as particles of dust float down through the air. The house is silent.

"Did something happen to him in the house?" Brielle asks, wanting to keep Rizette talking. At the sound of her voice, Rizette breaks her statuesque pose and leans back in the chair.

"I…" She hesitates again. "I get illogical ideas, I think from being here for so long. It's not the house, because if it was, he would be here with me."

"What do you mean?"

"We all have our vices, Miss Panya." Rizette runs her index finger along the edge of the desktop in front of her. "There came a time when I rarely saw him without a cigarette between his fingers and a bottle in his other hand."

"And you believe that had something to do with this house?"

"No, not really," Rizette says, her voice thin. "We bought the house thinking we'd have a family here. I wonder if, without the empty rooms, he would've been less haunted."

"That must've been tough," Brielle says inadequately. Comforting words have always been difficult for her to come by. She feels empathy for the woman, she wishes she knew how to relieve the pain of the past, but grief is a specific condition for which there is no universal remedy.

Rizette nods. "That's the way life is sometimes, right?" She wears a rueful smile. "You try and you try for something, you put all your heart and soul into it, but the reality is that dreams are an immaterial currency. Despite what we want to believe, no amount of desire can guarantee an outcome."

A desperate sadness has overcome the innkeeper's face. Her eyebrows draw together and upward in the middle. The weight of memories pulls at the corners of her mouth. She continues running her finger along the edge of the desk as if hoping she can clean away some invisible dust that's settled there. Brielle marvels at how opaque the spirit is, how grounded in this world. If she hadn't known better she might've reached out to touch the woman, place a comforting hand on her shoulder. But she knows she would pass right through her if she tried. She has no comfort to give but her words.

"Barney succumbed to lung cancer," Rizette says, her eyes glassy. "It was painful, but mercifully short."

"I'm sorry to hear that," Brielle whispers.

"Me too." For Rizette, the sadness is still fresh. "I couldn't bring myself to perform anymore—my sets became depressing. Andrew told me I kept bumming out the patrons, begged me to play the favorites, but I didn't have them in me. Besides, clubs like that were going out of fashion anyway—that was no longer the music of the day. I handed in my resignation less than a month after Barney was gone.

"I thought about leaving this house, but I couldn't. It had been my home for so many years at that point. Moving alone felt like an overwhelming task. Like admitting defeat. Not only was I leaving those empty rooms behind, but I would be leaving Barney as well."

She pauses and her finger stops, poised as if pointing to a particular place on a map.

"The mind is funny," she muses, smiling at Brielle. "So few of the memories here were good memories, and yet I still didn't want to leave them. It felt like speaking ill of the dead."

Brielle understands. She nods, feeling a twisting knot in her stomach as she does so. Why do so many feel that instinctual need?

"I began running this place as a bed and breakfast instead." Rizette stands suddenly. "I filled those rooms myself, the only way I knew how, and the company kept me from descending into madness. There was always another task, you see. Always some need to tend to. Another towel, a burnt-out light bulb, breakfast in the morning, lunch, and then supper. The trees needed pruning. I did it all myself, you know."

"All of it?"

"Oh, it wasn't so hard." She waves a dismissive hand. "Time consuming, yes. But that's what I wanted, wasn't it?"

Brielle imagines seventy-year-old Rizette riding a lawn mower and finds that it's not hard at all to envision.

"I still found time for my own vices," Rizette whispers. She steps away from the desk, turning her back on Brielle. Perplexed, Brielle wonders where the innkeeper is going and if she should follow. "I couldn't fix everything with detergent and a new bulb. I'd go weeks of feeling fine and then there'd be several hazy days where I'm surprised no visitor ever told me off."

"How do you mean?" Brielle stands, her chair emitting a high groan as it scrapes along the floor.

Rizette gestures with a tilt of her head toward the back corner of the room. Brielle's eyes flicker to the closet door. It's been closed this entire time, half hidden by the border of cabinets and bookshelves around the room.

"It's where I hid my liquor," Rizette says, letting Brielle in on a devastating secret. Her eyes have welled up again, and yet she doesn't stop moving ever closer to the door. "After serving supper I'd retire to this room and drink myself into a sobbing mess. I'd drink to the loss of the family I never had, and to the memory of my husband. In a perverted way, I felt closer to him by indulging in one of the ways in which he slowly destroyed himself. We couldn't speak much at the end of his life, but if I soaked myself in alcohol I could almost pretend he was there with me. Some nights, I never made it up to my bed. I'd awake the next morning in this closet, in pain from sleeping on a hard floor and drinking my eyes shut.

"I think that's how I died," she says, and reaches out a hand to pull the door open. The hinges are rusty and loud, announcing to the room that she's entered. Silent tears roll freely down her face, shimmering rivers in the light.

Brielle steps slowly around the desk. She holds out placating hands, asking Rizette to stop retreating. "Why do you say that?"

"Because it's where I find myself at the start of every damn day."

And with that, Rizette steps inside the closet and pulls the door closed.

"Wait!" Brielle pleads. She rushes the rest of the way, not finished asking her questions. The handle is cold when her fingers wrap around it. She twists, but it doesn't budge. Locked without a degree of give. Brielle tries for a few seconds more before giving up and knocking with the heel of her palm. "Rizette? Please, Rizette. I'm sorry if I chased you away. I only have a few more questions. Please, come back out. I just want to help you."

But there comes no response. No sound. No movement. Nothing to show that the spirit was there with her at all. Brielle backs away, feeling intense frustration. Just like the night before, she has a suspicion that she won't be seeing Rizette again until the next morning. Any inquiries will have to wait until then.

Mind churning through incoherent thoughts, Brielle turns to leave the office. The innkeeper may no longer be of any help tonight, but perhaps she can find Parrish.

She steps out into the hall. All the other lights in the house have gone dark. And somehow even the lights in the office are out now too. She stands in an unknowable emptiness, willing her eyes to adjust quickly before she moves again.

A loud metallic groan sounds in the darkness. The house voicing its displeasure. Brielle looks through the open doorway back into the office, but as far as she can tell, the closet hasn't opened again.

Then she turns her eyes to the ceiling, staring into the open space above her head. Her ears strain for further noises. Her breaths come shallow. Quiet. Not wanting to mask what could be a delicate clue.

Clicking. Something is clicking.

Brielle squints, reluctantly acknowledging that this might be the best her vision gets in the absence of light. She takes her first step down the hall, toward where the noise is coming from.

The clicking continues. No—not clicking. Pattering, like rain. A trickle. Droplets falling.

Ahead.

Brielle squints harder and thinks she can sense movement in the shadows. The sound emanates from the circular staircase leading up to the second floor. A steady trickle. Droplets landing on the floor tiles. She can maybe see them now—or is that her eyes playing tricks on her? No, she's close enough to see the stairwell. Close enough to see the droplets falling through the center of the spiral. But the rain is much too dark to be water. Is that just because *everything* is too dark at the moment? She's afraid to know that answer. Already, she thinks the air might smell faintly of iron. A metallic odor that accompanies the macabre. Standing at the threshold where the wood flooring gives way to the tiles, she can no longer deny the smell. It is pungent and chilling and yet somehow alluring.

Brielle reaches into her pocket, retrieving her phone. Without taking her eyes off the dark droplets, she swipes down from the top of the glass screen. A menu drops with shortcuts to some of the phone's features. Using her right thumb, she selects the flashlight. Immediately, the bright white bulb illuminates, flooding the stairwell before her.

The scene is bathed in scarlet. Raining down from above, collected in a puddle beneath the center of the spiral, spreading outward along the grout lines. All of it deep, shining, red, red blood.

Brielle backs away, inhaling sharply. The hand not holding the phone goes to cover her mouth. She turns away, heart hammering inside her. The investigation has elevated to a threatening level she wasn't prepared for—one she wouldn't have chosen. She's had ample experience with ghosts before. They make sudden movements. They might disappear and reappear at will. And the form they take might be unsettling at times. But ghosts do not have blood. And very rarely do ghosts have the ability to draw blood.

Brielle stumbles back down the hallway, using the light of her phone to guide her. Shadows move, hiding from the harsh illumination. Playing tricks on her eyes. The house creaks, but she cannot tell if it wants her to get away or if it means to betray her location so the darker forces may find her. Paintings swing on their nails as she passes. The walls grumble.

The muffled voice of an angry man sounds from the upper level.

The best thing to do when you are unprepared to face the level of haunting is to leave.

She wraps her fingers around the knob and yanks on the front door, but it doesn't budge. Brielle quickly checks the locks but neither is engaged. The chain hangs unused in its holder. She can see a distorted vision of the darkness beyond through the mottled, colored glass. She tries again, wrapping both hands around the knob, twisting and tugging with all her strength. The house howls at her and the door does not move. Again she tries, a sharper pull this time. Then with one foot against the wall. No success.

Defeated, Brielle backs away from the door. Her ears ring, listening for the sounds of the aging wood and plaster around her. The house has gone silent, knowing she's accepted her failure. Even the sound of dripping from the end of the corridor is gone. Is she too far away, or has the rain of blood ceased?

Brielle wills herself to calm down, forcing slow and measured breaths. She goes to the office door, hoping to barricade herself in a space with only one entry and exit. Neither door budges, and she remembers how resolute they'd stood the night before. Rizette's spirit is somewhere inside, but she doubts the innkeeper will answer her pleas for help.

Not wanting to travel any further down the hallway, Brielle turns to the living room. From where she stands, she can see the shape of the fireplace directly across from her, the wooden mantlepiece decorated with an arrangement of trinkets. She can only make out one of them in the darkness: a beer stein with gold plating around the base. Everything else in the room is blocked out by the doorframe.

Brielle crosses the corridor. She'd had to put away her phone to get a proper grip on the front door, and now she wonders whether she shouldn't take it back out again. But there is less need for it in the sitting room. The wide window, as always, invites the moonlight through the weathered glass.

The woman in the bloodied nightgown stands beside it. She stares out, her pale face barely registering the light of the moon, just as bedraggled and injured as the night before, though tonight she exudes a calmer aura. It's almost as though she's admiring the night sky, the black trees swaying beneath the inky darkness. Longing in the way she lingers.

Brielle watches her, trying not to make a noise, not wanting to disturb the spirit's peace. Her back is to one side of the doorframe, using it to hold steady, letting the image of the dripping blood wash away from her. Trying to determine if she should chance another encounter with the woman. Things would be so much easier if she could talk to Brielle, explain what she's doing here and what she remembers.

Tell her if there is a more nefarious entity present.

She takes one step forward and the house seizes the opportunity to let out a conspicuous creak. Calling to the woman. Letting her know that someone watches.

The spirit faces Brielle with the same reddened eyes both seeing and looking through her. For a moment she looks contrite and mournful. There's fear there, yes, but also a sadness that Brielle feels sinking within her like a warm swallow of whiskey. Then the spirit opens her mouth wide—wider than any living human could—and begins to scream. Her face morphs, more gaping mouth than anything else. A round black tunnel of rotted flesh.

Brielle stares, unable to avert her gaze, as the scream consumes her. There are no sounds from the house. No groans, no sighs. Nothing but the agonized scream implanting itself in her mind.

She has no idea how long it lasts—second, minutes, maybe more. Then the specter disappears altogether, vanishing faster than her scream can die. In her wake, it fades from the audible like a new coat of dust and all is silent once more, save for the distant rumble of a car as it drives off into the trees.

Moonlight bathes the floor before the wide window, but there's no sign that the woman was there. Brielle lets her gaze wander the room, but everything is as it should be. As it's been since she arrived at Garrick. She lets out short, gasping breaths and turns away, suddenly very tired. She tries the front door one last time, but it remains immobile.

Accepting that she will not be leaving tonight, Brielle slides toward her room with her back firmly against the hallway wall. In the stairwell, all is still, but the pool of blood lies dark across the tiles. She'd half hoped it would vanish along with the woman in the window. Of course, the worst things never disappear. They wait in the dark to be reckoned with. But if she can help it, that'll wait until tomorrow.

Holding her breath, Brielle shuffles quickly the rest of the way, throwing herself through the bedroom door and slamming it behind her.

As she undresses, Brielle contemplates the face of the woman in her mind. The sadness she saw there. The regret. Not just for having died, but for the circumstances that keep her here. This is not just an angry spirit, but a sad one as well. And if she's not the one keeping the others here, then Brielle is not anxious to find out what is.

WHEN WINTER COMES

Brielle spends the next hour wondering how she will fall asleep, only to find a new day awaiting her on the other side of a blink. She awakens feeling rested. And can't remember having any dreams at all, which is a surprise given the nightmarish images from the night before. Sunlight radiates through the gap in her curtains—thick, floral draperies she's yet to open. She tiptoes over to the bathroom to bathe and relieve herself.

It's only after brushing her teeth and a shower that she feels willing to venture out into the rest of the house. Pulling her hair back into an adequate bun, she exits into the hallway. Pale light streams through the colored glass in the front door and through the archway into the living room. The house groans its welcome, and Brielle responds by absentmindedly shifting her weight from one foot to the other.

She has to face the stairwell.

After taking a slow, deep breath, Brielle turns. She expects a scene of gore—blood spattered on the walls, a pool of scarlet covering the tiled floor—but this is not the sight that greets her.

Instead, she finds the stairwell clean. Well, maybe clean is not the correct word. It's just as old as the rest of the house, fallen victim to the cracks and fadings of age. But the blood is gone. Instead, it's the same burnt yellow as before, the wooden banister curling up and out of sight.

Her lips a thin, straight line, Brielle's hand comes to rest on the wide doorframe, staring down at the clean floor in bewilderment. Had she imagined the whole thing? It was dark and the sudden change in the house's atmosphere could have confused her. But she doesn't think that was likely. She's been in stressful situations before—ghosts can be dramatic, and some take every opportunity to catch you off guard. She'd been attentive, but not delusory. Plus, she'd turned on her flashlight and the liquid had definitely been red.

No. Whatever entity had done this had also made the blood vanish. It was a trick to frighten her. She wouldn't let it get in her way.

Brielle mounts the steps, climbing up into the light of the frosted amber windows. Between the blood dripping from the upper floor and Parrish and Rizette's reluctance to ascend, she's certain whatever needs confronting must come from above. Her fingers trace the banister, pleased by the smoothness of the polish. Even after all these years, the house retains some of its charm.

And then she notices it: a single streak of blood at the base of the wall where it meets the fourth step. The streak is so thin and small that she might've missed it, but Brielle has learned to search for such details—and this one brings her a great deal of calm. She was not hallucinating after all. On the contrary, she'd been very alert.

On the second floor, she briefly tries Laurel's door again. It's locked, same as yesterday, so she moves on. There must be something up here she's missed. Something that might tell her about the woman in the window. After all, the sounds had begun up here.

Last night, when she'd left Rizette's office, she'd been standing in the middle of the hallway by the front door when she heard the first phantom creaks. That would be beneath the far end of the hallway—the window over the porch. Brielle hurries down the corridor, her footsteps feeling louder than normal in the morning quiet. She reaches the window in no time and begins a more thorough search, running her eyes and her fingers along the frame. Nothing but chipping paint and deterioration. A line of mold along the right side of the window frame. No signs of the woman or anything that looks like it might be of import. She can come back if something else arises, but for the time being it seems the window has no effect on the spiritual happenings.

After a more thorough search of the second-floor bathroom and unoccupied bedroom, Brielle still has nothing to show for her efforts. There's nothing particularly special about either of them. Nothing that draws the mind, that elicits an emotional response. Reluctantly, she decides to move on, knowing that she doesn't have the time to linger this morning. She returns to her bedroom and packs her sparse belongings. The process takes under a minute, and by the time she's swung the duffel bag over her shoulder, you might never have known she'd been there.

Just the way she likes it.

As Brielle strides purposefully past the office, however, her step falters.

The doors are open again, now that the morning has come. She peers in. Everything looks exactly as she'd left it the day before: shelves of knickknacks, the armchair behind the desk, the old green lamp with the bronze pull chain. She walks in, shoes knocking softly on the floor. Her hand slides over the guestbook, feeling the timeworn leather cover. How many names are present? Hundreds, she would imagine. So many potential screaming ghost women to choose from. The pages feel brittle, dried from exposure to decades of stale air. Her fingers skim palimpsest so bold she might've been able to read some of the names without looking. But she does look, her gaze sliding over the distinct handwriting of a dozen or so past visitors.

Melissa V.

Ernest Lee

Gregory Alba

She flips through a few more pages of guests, some who came back before leaving to scribble a note of thanks, some who didn't even put their full name.

Amy Lynn – Those muffins were amazing! Thanks again!

S. Toren

Parrish Creed

"I was so close to finishing that notebook." Rizette enters the room. Brielle rips her eyes away from the pointed signature. The innkeeper looks calm, pensive, in the exact condition as the day before. "There were only a handful of pages left. Of course, it doesn't *really* matter, but it would've been nice."

"Did everyone sign?"

"Everyone who stayed here," Rizette says with a nod. Then she tilts her head. "I'm sorry, I know that I know you, but I can't quite remember who you are."

"Brielle." She's unfazed by the lapse in memory. With repetition, they'll find it easier to remember her.

"Ah, yes, you are helping us."

"I'm doing what I can, at least."

"If there's anything I can do to help…"

"You've already done so much."

"Have I?"

Rizette seems bemused by the idea that she's already provided support. She smiles vacantly as she crosses her arms.

Brielle leans back against the edge of the desk, hands resting on the tabletop. As she relaxes into a more casual pose, the house seems to settle around them. The walls creak, and in response, the pipes groan as if imploring the walls to quiet down. They wouldn't want to miss a word of her speech. Brielle is aware of all this and raises her eyes to the ceiling, waiting for things to calm again. When the noises cease, she returns to her conversation. "Actually, since you're here, maybe you can answer something for me. When does Laurel emerge?"

"He can't be reached now. It's not his time."

"Yes, I know it's not his time, but when does his time begin?"

"He won't be back until the afternoon, I'm afraid."

"Oh," Brielle says. She looks down at her watch. It's just past nine thirty in the morning. She'd better leave now if she doesn't want to be late. "I suppose I'll have to speak with him later."

"Don't worry. He'll be back. We always come back."

"That's the issue," Brielle mutters under her breath. Then, louder, "I'm going out today."

Rizette eyes the bag on her shoulder. "You're leaving us?"

"Just until the afternoon. Hopefully everyone will be around by then."

I shouldn't be leaving.

"But you're taking your things."

"I don't think I need to stay here overnight anymore. I've seen Salma's ghost already."

And whatever else is hiding in the shadows.

Without waiting for a response, she turns to leave. Rizette watches from the doorway of the office as Brielle opens the front door.

She's probably wondering if I'm chasing a lead, Brielle thinks, guilt coursing through her veins. She'd promised to set the spirits free. Not even forty-eight hours later she's packed up all her things and is prepared to go galivanting to another town for lunch with an ex-roommate. That doesn't feel very much like the actions of a dedicated mind, but Brielle reminds herself that it's only one day—and a partial day at that. She's never interrupted a job before, but she's also rarely this close to a good friend.

If I took this job to clear my mind, why am I running from it?

She leaves the Garrick Estate and rides US-1 north out of Camden and up the Maine coastline. Trees line the way, a mixture of evergreen and bare deciduous. This late in the year, snow could fall at any time. She's never weathered a New England winter, and hopes this won't be the first. She'd hate to get snowed in at Garrick.

In less than half an hour, the highway dumps her out in Belfast. Brielle follows the GPS as it takes her through a quaint downtown area—squat brick buildings neatly assembled beside the road, storefronts shaded by striped canvas awnings. The coffee shop isn't difficult to find, and given how few people there are, she doesn't need to drive very far to find parking.

Brielle shuts off the engine and sits in silence, trying to shoo away the tremors of anxiety in her stomach. She has no reason to be nervous—she knows this. Vivian isn't the type to hide emotions. If she'd been angry at Brielle, she wouldn't have agreed to see her. Simple as that. But even though they lived together for four years in college, Brielle is still somewhat afraid to meet face to face again.

After all, things change—people change. And what if they aren't as agreeable as they'd been before?

Sitting there thinking won't do anything but make Vivian wait. Brielle gets out of the car and walks steadily down the sidewalk.

Café D'amis is painted in curling letters over the image of a pink donut. Cute and classy. Brielle pulls the door open and steps inside.

Dark wooden bookshelves and local artwork cover the brick walls. Plants in painted ceramic pots hang amid strings of fairy lights. Bossa nova plays through hidden speakers. The warm aroma of roasting coffee. The café's interior is half full of twenty-somethings and a few people her age including a black woman by herself at a table for two in the far corner.

Brielle is pulled to her friend by gravity, and when she's no more than a few paces away, Vivian notices her.

"Bri!" she exclaims, standing immediately. Her embrace is just as firm as Brielle remembers it. They spend a few minutes exchanging meaningless banter about how good the other looks and it's yet another reminder of just how long it's been since they'd last seen each other. Vivian is wearing fewer accessories these days. She'd never been one for makeup, but she was known to don a dozen bits and bobs at any given time. When Brielle points this out, Vivian laughs, declaring the jewelry kept breaking and she kept not replacing it. They order drinks—Brielle an americano and Vivian a cappuccino. Neither can resist the temptation to accompany this with a chocolate croissant. The minutes melt away, and gradually, Brielle forgets why she was so hesitant to reconnect with her friend. Perhaps it's just her frequent worry that time spent apart from anyone means your paths have diverged, that their growth won't be in tandem to your own. But she forgets that separated vines can still grow intertwined once more when reintroduced. Vivian moved to Belfast take care of her ailing mother, and selfish as it seems now, Brielle had expected this to drastically change her friend's demeanor. Luckily, it appears her assumptions have been incorrect.

When they start receiving subtle glares from the wait staff for having occupied such a coveted seat without keeping up a steady stream of purchases, Vivian and Brielle decide to make their way to the second location, both surprisingly hungry despite the generous size of their breakfast pastries. The aroma of coffee is replaced by savory smells—tomatoes and mushrooms and cooked greens. They're fortunate enough to claim a table by the window with a view of the small park across the way. Nothing much but grass, trees, and a low fence decorated by painted ceramic flowers.

"Do you ever miss the old days?" Vivian says, contemplating her sandwich when it arrives. "God, I miss college."

Brielle snorts. She didn't miss a beat unwrapping and diving into her own food, so she does this through a mouthful. "Endless studying and stress? I think your rearview mirror might be a little rose-colored."

"Well, yeah, of course it was stressful and a lot of hard work, don't get me wrong." Vivian takes a bite and then chews pensively. "I guess, I mean the *feel* of college, you know? It was all about discovery. It was about newness. About figuring out who you were away from your childhood and your parents and all the people you were reliant on not just physically but emotionally."

"That experience might've been particular to you," Brielle says. "We were only twenty minutes from my folks, remember?"

"Yeah, I suppose. I don't know." Vivian seems suddenly melancholy, and Brielle wonders if it would've been easier just to agree with her than to see what's happened to her friend now. She's not sad, per se, but her happiness is tainted. Her enthusiasm has already begun to wane from a few hours ago. "I guess it's an atmosphere I find myself chasing every now and then. At least once a year," she says, laughing. "I'm like the goddamn seasons. Every winter I start thinking about how good things used to be."

Her laughter dies.

"It's hard to leave the past behind, especially when the present isn't any better. Everything, my art…it felt fresher then. It felt like I had more to say. There was depth. There were questions. There was the *unknown*." She raises her eyebrows as she says the last word. "Now, it's all big and bold brush strokes."

Brielle has no idea what she means, but then again she's never been a creative. She can't relate to what it must feel like to derive joy from your own artistic output, and to have only yourself to blame for its absence.

"Look at that!" Vivian says, gesturing at the park across the way. Among the floral sculptures affixed to the low fence is a large sunflower with brilliant yellow petals. "It's bright, it's symmetrical. It's…uninteresting. There's no nuance to a sunflower's beauty."

"But why should beauty be restricted to nuance?" Brielle frowns and Vivian sighs.

Lunch comes and goes, and yet again the two find themselves at the end of passive stares by the wait staff. Brielle is surprised how much time has passed, and that she's still reluctant to leave. She's forgotten what spending time with Vivian is like—breezy and quick, as if some creature is stealing the numbers from the clock while they aren't looking. She'd sought an escape by taking the Garrick job, but instead she's found it here with her college roommate. The idea had never crossed her mind when planning the trip.

They vacate their seats in the restaurant and decide, nonverbally, to stroll down Church Street, dipping lithely in and out of silly and serious topics.

"I actually hope I never have potato leek soup again," Vivian concludes, after recounting her foray into "bulk cooking" in order to save time. Without first checking the number of servings made by one recipe, she'd accidentally produced enough soup to allegedly feed all of Belfast. "If my mom wasn't absolutely dead-set on never wasting a single crumb—"

"How's your mom doing, by the way?" Brielle asks.

"Oh, you know. Same old. She's adamant about *accidentally* using my dead name every so often," Vivian says. Her tone is light, but her expression is steeped in frustration. "Actually, it's incredibly annoying—and rude, given I'm the one who volunteered to take care of her. But she'd rather insult her trans daughter and risk isolation than change. I'm thinking I might just leave. If Antony doesn't want a go, then we can find the money for a home. She can get better care from someone she's paying to insult."

Brielle laughs.

"I'm being serious, Bri. I'm getting close to the end of my rope."

"Yeah, but she's your mom."

"That doesn't really matter."

"You don't think blood makes a difference?"

"No, I don't." Vivian might be the most serious Brielle has ever seen her. She's staring off at the far end of the street, her mouth a straight line. "Clinging to blood comes from tribe mentality. And tribe mentality only works if both parties are actually trying to protect one another. If someone wants to hurt me, why should I cling to them in the name of blood? How are they any different from some bigot off the street?"

Brielle's instinct is to argue, but she finds that she can't. She knows Vivian's views on family are different than most people's. She had to deal with a lot more strife growing up—a lack of familial support that some take for granted.

"I guess they aren't."

Vivian shakes her head. "I'm tired of surrounding myself with people who think little of me. It would be one thing if she apologized or even just changed her behavior. But all she does is make these half-hearted excuses for forgetting, as if I didn't come out twelve years ago."

"People aren't perfect, you know?" Brielle hates to see Vivian hating her family. It feels like such a lonely state.

"Yeah, but they still have to try."

"I'm sorry," Brielle says, and slips her arm into her friend's. "I'd probably feel the same."

A large flower box hangs from the sill of a second-story window. Verdant and overgrown, it creates a canopy of foliage which hangs over the sidewalk. Vivian lifts one hand, sliding her fingertips across the underside of the leaves.

"So," Brielle says, her voice low. "I hate to bring this up, but are you—"

"Yes," Vivian says, withdrawing her outstretched hand suddenly. Her shoulders tense up, not in anger but in wariness. Preparation. It's a learned habit that Brielle recognizes from their past arguments. "Ben and I are not together."

Brielle breathes a sigh of relief. "Sorry, I just had to make sure."

"You know he wasn't all bad, right?"

"Viv—"

"He's taken some anger management courses—did a ton of mindfulness exercises."

"Are you communicating with him?"

"I'm just saying, he is one of the people taking steps to better themselves." She brushes her hair back, every part of her body language still tense. Her relationship with Ben was always a source of abrasion in their otherwise genial friendship. "I believe in him. *But* I haven't forgotten the past. You don't need to be so worried."

But she is.

Vivian changes the subject. "How's your mom doing?"

Brielle clears her throat. "She died, actually. A few days ago."

"Oh no, Bri! That's horrible. I'm so sorry."

"Thanks," Brielle says. She thinks about waving the concern away, but why should she lie to her friend. "It's pretty fresh. I never forget that she's gone or anything, I just…am not sure what to do with it. You know? That knowledge."

"I know you two had a rocky relationship, but in the end you were good, right?"

"Yeah," Brielle says. They walk in silence for several minutes until Church Street becomes a tributary for a larger vein through the town. Unsurprisingly, the sun—just visible between the layers of clouds—has already begun its descent. Something in her mind tells Brielle that she ought to start heading back to the house. She can't put off her duties much longer.

"People are so odd when it comes to death," she says. "I know people must've gossiped about my mom—everyone gets mentioned now and again when they're not around—but now that she died, all anyone can say is that she was some perfect and polished angel."

"Of course," Vivian says with a chuckle. "Nobody wants to speak ill of the dead."

"But why not? It isn't as though you can erase their mistakes by not mentioning them."

"Yeah, but does it fix anything to bring them up?"

"I haven't decided yet," Brielle says absently. "It might."

"Are you going to give a eulogy at her funeral?"

"I don't know that I'm the right person to do that."

"You talk about forgiveness and family, Bri. Your mom *did* try. She's one of the few. I'd kill for mine to do the same."

"I know." Brielle suddenly doesn't want to talk much anymore. In fact, she's ready to get back in her car to return to Camden. The air is too cold, the streets too unfamiliar. Perhaps she's still better suited to measured bouts of company. "And I loved her for that. It just feels wrong for people to say she's something she wasn't."

"So, are you alright?" Vivian asks.

"Yeah," Brielle admits with a nod. "A little sad, but what else is new?"

"Ain't that the truth." Vivian snorts. "You get so used to sadness, you forget what happiness feels like."

"No, I never forget. I think that's my problem: I know happiness is there somewhere. I just can't find it."

They stop at the corner but don't turn around. Not just yet. Brielle can feel Vivian watching her, making some sort of assessment. Is it sympathy? Pity? They're no longer arm in arm, and her left side feels suddenly cold—colder even than the side that hadn't been close to Vivian.

"What are you doing here?" her friend asks. "I mean, your mom just passed away and the funeral hasn't happened yet. What are you doing all the way in Maine?"

"I told you, I took a job—"

"I know, but why?"

Brielle shakes her head, suddenly frustrated. When had their visit gone from a much-needed break to a psychoanalysis?

"I needed to get away, alright?" she says, aware but unable to stop herself from being so aggravated. "That's my problem, remember? I don't cling to my problems, I run away from them."

"Running away from the same issue is just another form of clinging to the past," Vivian says gently. She places a comforting hand on Brielle's upper arm, and though Brielle's instinct is to pull away, she forces herself not to. Reluctantly, she feels her frustration ebbing.

"I guess we all have our own seasons."

A WINDOW INTO THE PAST

What has become increasingly clear is that Brielle cannot gather all the information from within the Garrick Estate. Not only because the ghosts don't remember enough of the details to secure their release but because Brielle is running out of mobile data. Without proper Internet, she is frustratingly cut off.

She decides to rent a motel room.

Her visit with Vivian in Belfast lasted much longer than she'd anticipated. And by the time she returns to Camden, evening has fallen and the world is dark. She orders a to-go salad from the same diner where she'd had lunch the day before, then finds the closest motel to the Garrick Estate with adequate Wi-Fi. It's an ill-kempt, ramshackle place with peeling paint and a half-missing sign. The missing portion, she's told by the man at the desk, has been stolen again by mischievous teenagers, who have a habit of trading possession of it. It will turn up again in the parking lot sooner or later, but in less than a fortnight it will be gone once more.

Brielle smiles and nods through the entire retelling of this fabled tiff, not asking any questions for fear of elongating the tale.

When the old man has finally exhausted his version of the saga, he hands her the key and she swiftly departs. Now that she's back in Camden, she feels a burning desire to forge onward.

In her motel room, Brielle opens her laptop. She spends the next few hours scouring the Internet. But much to her chagrin, her search comes up empty. The Garrick Estate is just not noteworthy enough to have garnered any attention, it seems. Inane article follows inane article, until Brielle is about ready to hurl her laptop through the motel window. Instead, she pushes the computer away and closes her eyes, forcing herself to take several deep breaths. The Internet is an easy resource for most topics, but she reminds herself that it's incomplete. In obscure places, things don't make the Internet until someone puts them there. It doesn't mean nothing happened; it just means the rest of the country didn't take note.

Which also means that if she wants to know about something in particular, her best bet is probably the city library. By the time she admits defeat, the clock reads nearly midnight. She sleeps, happy not to have Salma's screams in her ears, or the sight of dripping blood.

~

In the morning, Brielle makes sure to get an early start. The library is close enough—most things in Camden are—and she arrives ten minutes after opening at a gorgeous brick building with immaculate landscaping. Several species of colorful flowers flank the path, which leads up a few steps to the entrance, nestled amid a semicircle of roman columns. This place has history, Brielle is sure of it—though, most towns on the east coast do. It makes her wonder if, had her local library been designed with a similarly unique layout, she would've taken more interest in going as a child. Entering this building, which has been carved out of the hillside with winding pathways through abundant foliage, would've inspired ideas of adventure and mystery. When she was a young girl, the library seemed boring and dingy—a large, dirty room in a square brick building. She liked the reading but not the package. Mother used to walk her there. Kam on one hand and Brielle on the other. For every ten books they read each summer, they would go see a movie at the cinema. Sunny days full of reading and theater snacks. Perhaps that's why she still associates the smell of worn pages with that of buttery popcorn. When had the tradition stopped?

Inside, she's greeted by a familiar hushed silence and a cozy reading area. Tall windows look out over the harbor. Gray skies and a grayer tide. She wonders how soon it'll be until first snowfall.

"May I help you?" a woman asks, approaching Brielle from behind.

Brielle smiles. "Yes, I was wondering if you kept an archive of local newspapers."

The librarian, a kind-looking woman aging gracefully into her golden years, nods. "We do," she says proudly. "The *Camden Herald* has been reporting in this community for almost a hundred and fifty years. We have a fair number of well-preserved issues, especially those dating from the Great Depression onward."

"Are visitors allowed to view them?"

"They're on rolls. But you can use the machine while supervised."

Brielle agrees, asking for a sampling of years from the late 1980s to the early 1990s, which is when she assumes the Garrick house would've stopped operating as a bed and breakfast, judging by the décor. The librarian leads Brielle downstairs to where most of the books are kept. A dozen patrons already roam the stacks, perusing the shelves with determined aplomb. Are any of them aware of the Garrick Estate? Are tales about the haunted dwelling as common of knowledge among the residents of the town as she'd initially been led to believe? Given the absence of Internet material—not even one social media post that she could find referring to the house in any form—she finds it hard to believe. But then who had given Nadine so much grief about the house being haunted?

The librarian leads her into a side room and the rest of the people disappear.

In the center, a handful of clustered desks contain ancient-looking machines. Brielle immediately recognizes the computer for viewing microfilm, having used several in her line of work. Before the woman can instruct her to do so, she wanders over and plops herself down in front of the bulging screen.

"I'll go ahead and grab them," the librarian says, striding over to a metal cabinet. "By the way, I'm Glenda."

"Brielle." She powers on the machine, waiting patiently as the lamp warms up.

"Seems like you know what you're doing."

"I've used a few of these through my work."

"And what is it you do?"

"I rid places of ghosts," Brielle says bluntly. She's comfortable telling the truth, finding workarounds to be tiresome and confusing—especially when it comes to requesting research material. Why try to keep a story straight when she can simply lay out the facts? As such, she's used to all manner of responses. None of them surprise her anymore.

Glenda laughs a little, assuming that she's joking, but when Brielle doesn't join in, she glances at her from the cabinet. "Ghosts?" is all she says.

"Yeah," Brielle replies. "If people are being haunted, they hire me to find resolution for the spirits."

The woman seems hesitant, though she withdraws her hands from the cabinet, clutching six small black boxes of microfilm. "And does it...require some type of spell?"

At this, Brielle does laugh. "Not usually. I'm not a witch or anything. It's typically just figuring out what happened to them, what's keeping them here, and then fixing the problem."

Glenda sets the boxes down beside Brielle, her mouth slightly open. She seems to want to say more but is hesitant. Whereas she'd been perfectly amiable before, now she's wary. She's careful not to make too much eye contact.

"So that brought you to Camden." It's not a question.

Brielle is suddenly struck by the idea that this woman might know about the Garrick house. "Do you—"

But Glenda holds up a hand to stop her. "Please," she says. "I don't want to know."

With that, she makes to leave the room.

"Aren't you supposed to supervise me?" Brielle asks. Not that she wants the librarian hovering over her, but she hates to leave someone feeling uneasy.

"You know what you're doing," Glenda says simply as she reaches the door. She doesn't look back. "I'll trust that you won't steal anything. Let me know on your way out that you've finished."

~

Brielle spends several hours combing through the newspaper pages, sliding past scan after black-and-white scan. None of which do any more than paint a picture of a quiet, old city on the east coast. There are seasons of heavy snows, political campaigns, minor changes to historical sites, and even the odd story of random noteworthy residents. She sees very little in the way of tragic events. Her eyes begin to glaze over, and as she scrolls faster she has to remind herself that she is *looking* for specific content among the headlines and photos, and not just trying to get through each reel as quickly as possible.

Brielle makes it through the eighties without any results and pushes those boxes aside with palpable disappointment. Is she wasting her time here as well? Did each death in the Garrick house go unreported? She can imagine Rizette's death not eliciting a front-page story if, as the woman suspects, she ended her own life. But Laurel was fairly certain that he and his wife were murdered. Surely that sort of double horror spectacle would've shaken the town to its core.

By the time Brielle has entered 1992, she's convinced that there are no stories to be found. Nothing about the Garrick Estate that will be of any use to her. Once again, her eyes glaze over, and she sweeps from one page to next, barely scanning the images for the familiar house or the text for words that might pique her interest. Where will she look next? If not the Internet or the local newspaper, then what information remains? There must be somewhere else she can go. Someone to talk to. Laurel had said he had a daughter.

She nearly misses it, and has to go back a page once she realizes her mistake. Brielle's heart skips a beat. In the middle of November 1992, a headline screams out at her in bold, capitalized letters: *MURDER IN CAMDEN*. Without having read anything further, Brielle knows she's found what she's been looking for. She can feel it in her bones. The rush of satisfaction that she's familiar with, which marks the turning point in every case she's ever worked. Below the title, the Garrick house stares back at her in black and white. An artfully framed image taken from near the gate, such that the lantern above the address number sits level with the highest peak of the roof.

Brielle devours the article, which she's surprised to find is not as pristinely preserved as most of the other newspaper images she's been scanning. In several places, she has to squint—drawing her face closer to the screen to make out the words.

On November 16th, the old Garrick house—at that point long run by Rizette Colton as a cozy bed and breakfast—was the subject of a vicious homicide which claimed the lives of three people, including Rizette herself. The article is frustratingly mum on the details. It doesn't even name the other victims besides Rizette—only mentioning that they were guests at the time of the attack. It finishes by stating that the killer was still at large. Gone by the time authorities arrived. Brielle reads the article multiple times, afraid that she's skipped over more crucial details. But the story remains inadequate.

Still, it's not entirely useless, she thinks, sitting back in her chair. Now at least she knows Rizette, Laurel, and the woman in the window were killed in the same night. A triple homicide. In a town like this, she can see why that would earn the house a reputation for being haunted. There must be a record of a pursuit of the killer in the following editions. The police wouldn't have simply given up the search. Not with three victims.

Feeling a somewhat renewed sense of direction, Brielle scrolls to the next page.

Her eyes widen.

She scrolls to the next and feels the quickening in her pulse. A rush of adrenaline in her veins.

The pages are blank.

She continues, finding that while not every page is gone, the gaps continue. Most of them are front pages.

Brielle stops and again sits back in her chair, her mind churning through a thousand possibilities. She doubts the library knows, not with the woman at the helm seemingly so skittish about the possibility of anything untoward. As soon as Brielle asked for these years, she would've denied her.

No, this was done without the library's knowledge. Brielle briefly considers whether it could be coincidence, or the result of improper preservation. After all, why would someone erase these pages and leave the one about the incident itself?

Perhaps they were just inept?

She shakes her head, scrolling back to the first page with the article about the triple homicide. There are too many possibilities. Too many things she doesn't know and can't assume. The only thing she can be certain of is that a tragic event occurred the 16th of November, 1992, resulting in the deaths of Rizette, Laurel, and Salma.

Brielle gazes at the black-and-white photo of the Garrick Estate, her mind churning. The photographer must've been a fan of dramatization, what with their framing of the house and their decision to take the image at sunset. The lights are all on, creating an ethereal glow around the building. The windows are alive. Pale, where the silhouette of the house is dark. And as Brielle gazes, she feels another rush of excitement, wondering how on earth she'd failed to realize this very crucial detail as she'd stood before the house in person.

There is a third level.

THE CYCLE

Brielle's immediate desire is to rush back to the Garrick house, but she's been on enough jobs to know that the house isn't going anywhere anytime soon, and neither are the spirits inside. Besides, she unwittingly skipped lunch and her famished mind refuses to focus.

Reasoning that she's no use in her current state, Brielle drives to the local grocery store. She heads straight for the granola bars and microwave noodles, though she also tosses a few vegetables in her basket, along with a twelve-pack of fruity drinks that feel healthier than soda. When she enters the self-checkout, her phone rings.

"Hey, Brielle!"

"Kam," she says, shifting the phone to one shoulder so she can continue scanning items. "What's up?"

"Uh, not much," he says in an entirely unconvincing voice. One thing he's never been is a good liar. "Just wanted to see how things were going."

"And wondering if I'm still going to make the funeral in time?"

"The thought had crossed my mind."

"I'll be there," Brielle assures him. She feels irrationally irritated by his decision to check up on her, all thoughts of the job having left her mind. Even though she knows he doesn't mean anything incendiary by it, her mood has soured. "I said I would so I will."

"I know, I know," he says quickly, trying to deescalate the conversation. "I'll be here, so…just, yeah, I look forward to seeing you."

"Is that all?" she asks, hating how confrontational she sounds.

"There is one more thing," Kam says, then hesitates. "You don't have to decide now or even any time before the funeral really. I just thought you should know that I'm doing a eulogy, and if you want to do one too, you're welcome to."

Brielle's mouth becomes a thin line, her ire displaced almost as quickly as it came with a conflicted sadness. Vivian had asked her the same question. She hadn't had an answer then, and she still doesn't have one now. Words have left her, and though Brielle tries several times to respond to him, the obvious answer does not arrive. Instead, she lets out a long, slow breath.

"I'll think about it," she says eventually.

"That's all I ask," her brother replies.

She hangs up.

As she finishes packaging her food, Brielle again finds herself preoccupied. For all the death she's surrounded herself with, funerals have never been easy for her. They are strange celebrations—in the nominal sense—of the deceased. Often not at all centered around the actual dead person but what the attendees crave in their absence: a reason to gather, a reason to reminisce without seeming maudlin.

Again, it comes back to the polished memories and sanded edges, which tend to miss the fact that people have a natural roughness to them. Death doesn't erase that. But perhaps this is an idea she's more comfortable with only because she spends so much time with the dead. For her, it's not as sacred a space. There's no need for a determined politeness. In some ways, Brielle finds the more sanitized funerals diminish what made the deceased a real person. It's important to remember everything about them. After all, the front of a sticker is nice to look at, but if the back isn't adhesive, it's just a sheet of paper.

She shakes her head. Most people don't want to hear that opinion, and a funeral isn't just for her sake but theirs as well.

As she closes the trunk of her car, Brielle realizes her phone is still pressed firmly in her hand. The screen is lit, the touch of her palm having kept it awake, and her movements have navigated to the recent calls log. Beneath her brother's name and Vivian's is her call to Nadine made three days ago when Brielle left for Camden.

Nadine Toren, it reads, and Brielle decides, then and there, that before she goes back to Garrick, she has one more stop to make.

~

Nadine Toren lives in a normal-sized house near town. Wide white slats stretch between blue trim, and every window is flanked by navy shutters. A nice square lawn blankets the front yard, bordered by bushes with small round leaves. The stark contrast between this home and the Garrick house makes Brielle feel as though she's traveled more than the few miles to get from one to the other. She parks her Volkswagen in front and drifts through the open gate.

On the front porch, Nadine has hung a blue-and-green wind ornament that spins hypnotically in the breeze. Brielle's momentum carries her forward at a reckless pace.

She knocks five times on the front door.

A flurry of movement ensues from within, followed by indiscernible voices, before the door opens to the extent that its chain allows.

Nadine's eye takes a moment to recognize the woman in front of her.

"Brielle?" she says, surprised.

"I hope I haven't caught you at a bad time."

"There've been worse."

"Could I ask you a few things?"

"Right now?" Are those nerves in her voice?

"Yes, if you don't mind."

"Oh, sure. Sure." The door closes briefly while she undoes the chain. When it reopens, it swings wide. Nadine is wearing the same jacket as the last time Brielle saw her, with the picture of the moon on it. "Please come in."

She gestures for Brielle to follow her into the house. Brielle does so, closing the front door behind her with a soft click.

The heater has been running, making her wonder how Nadine can possibly wear a fleece layer, but she says nothing about it. Inside, the home is just as magazine-ready as the exterior. Everything begins with polished wooden floors that Brielle can tell are real and old. But despite their age, the floorboards are in remarkable condition. This is a house that has been kept well. The entryway, which opens unto the living room, is spacious, with a high ceiling and tall windows. Above, she can see several doors leading to other rooms, though all of these are shut.

"Please, have a seat," Nadine says, gesturing to the sofa. "I'll be right back."

She disappears up the stairs, and Brielle is treated to the sound of muffled voices again. She waits patiently, eyeing the furniture and décor. Every person's belongings tell a story about them—a painting as adequate as any visual medium. You just have to know how to interpret the strokes. Brielle is still working on this ability.

"Sorry about that," Nadine says, returning from the second floor. "Ten-year-olds. They never want to do their homework."

"I didn't know you had kids," Brielle says.

"Just the one. She has the strong will of three though."

Brielle laughs politely, eyes still roaming the room.

"Do you have any?" Nadine asks, though the look on her face says she expects a certain answer.

"No."

"Have you ever wanted any?"

Brielle thinks before responding. "I used to—or at least I thought I did. But when I got older, I realized it would probably be better for the both of us if I didn't."

"The both of us?"

"Me and the child."

Nadine nods. "I see."

"Some people shouldn't have children," Brielle says simply.

"That's true." Nadine sits in the armchair facing her. "But I'm sure that's not the thing you came to talk about. Have you, well, done it?"

"Gotten rid of the ghosts? No. They're still there."

"Oh."

"But I needed to ask you a few more questions," Brielle says, deciding where to begin. She crosses one leg over the other, hands clasped together to keep her appearance as neutral as possible. "Three questions, actually."

Despite Brielle's calm tone, her employer tenses. Her shoulders tighten and she straightens her back almost imperceptibly so. "Alright."

"Why did you *really* buy the inn? Why do you visit every night but refuse to enter? And why is your surname on the last page of the guestbook?"

Nadine freezes, obviously shocked. Brielle doesn't like to feel confrontational, but approaching the questions in a gentler manner would feel meandering. For a few long moments Nadine sits in the armchair, breathing steadily, frozen as the questions coalesce in her mind. She doesn't seem angry—Brielle doubted she would be, but there's always a small chance. If anything, there's a sadness behind her eyes. A regret.

"You're perceptive," she says finally.

"What did you hope I would discover?" Brielle asks, wondering if she should be insulted.

"To be honest, I was hoping you might just do some sort of ritual and the ghosts would be gone."

"It doesn't work that way."

Nadine sighs, and Brielle can tell that she's exhausted. Not simply in the way that a person might be exhausted at the end of a long work day, but as someone who spends a great deal of their time holding things back and cannot figure out how to let go. It's in the lines around her mouth, the discoloration around her eyes. She is withholding so many things that it's causing her physical discomfort.

"I was six when he brought me there," she says softly. Her eyes flicker up to the ceiling as if to make sure she isn't overheard. "Most of the memory is extremely fuzzy. I remember being strapped into the back of the station wagon and awaking to see the Garrick house appear out of the darkness. It was the scariest place I'd ever been.

"My father left me in the car and told me not to move while he went inside to take care of things. I didn't know what that meant, but nothing anybody did could make me want to go near that house. I stayed where I was, just like he said, and I stared up at the lit windows, wondering why he'd brought me to such a terrible place, and why he seemed so frantic.

"I waited. I don't know how long I was there—it felt like forever—but in hindsight, it couldn't have been more than fifteen minutes. I was cold and tired, I just wanted to go home. Nobody had explained anything to me. Then I saw movement in the front window. A person standing there looking down at the car. At first, I couldn't tell who it was because of the backlighting, but she moved and her face became clear. It was my mother."

Nadine pauses, the backs of her fingers pressed against her mouth. She's not crying—perhaps because she's too familiar with these wounds to cry anymore—but there is an intense sadness on her features even so.

"So, you mean, both of your parents went into the house," Brielle clarifies.

"No," Nadine says, frowning.

"Then how did your mother get inside?"

"She was already there."

It's at this moment that Brielle knows where the story is headed. The skin of her arms ripples, but she says nothing, wanting to hear the words from Nadine's mouth. Wanting to know her version of the story.

"She looked down at me and I could see her saying something, but I couldn't move. I sat in the car, staring back as she screamed in terror. I'll never forget the look on her face—the tears in her eyes, the blood, and the bruises already forming from an attack I hadn't seen. And I was so young. I was so, so young. All I could do was watch. The knife came out of nowhere. I barely even saw it before it was dragged across her throat. Then everything became a rain of blood. It splattered the window and drenched her nightgown. Everything. Her arms, the floor.

"I was too in shock at that moment to register what was going on, but I figured out later that it must've been my father. He never came back to the car. I waited there on my own for another ten minutes before the police showed up. Then everything became a sea of blue and red flashing lights."

Her gaze falls to her clasped hands.

Brielle tries not to let any emotions show through her voice. "And the police thought it was your father too?"

"Yes. At least, as far as I can tell."

"But they weren't sure?"

"Well, they never found him. He was never caught."

Should I tell her his ghost is also haunting the house? Brielle wonders. Which meant his body was probably hidden somewhere on the grounds.

"I went to the library this morning to check their catalog of preserved newspapers," she says. "There's the front-page article from when this happened, but nothing about the investigation or the search for your father. Do you know why that is?"

Nadine looks up at the ceiling again. "This house has been in my family for decades. My father and his parents spent all of their summers in Camden. They were rich, influential, and had friends in high places. From what I can guess, my grandfather knew the owner of the *Herald*. He didn't want my father's name in the paper—to keep people from harassing our family."

"So he had the archives cleansed of your father's name?"

"That would be my guess."

"After that night at the Garrick house, were you immediately taken in by your grandparents?"

Nadine nods.

Brielle feels a surge of pity for the woman. To have been so young and watched your mother die a gruesome death. That alone would've felt insurmountable. But for her father to have been the killer, the one who took her to the scene of the crime and left her, that's unbelievably worse. Cruel. Her life had been upended that night.

"I lived with my grandparents from then on, and we spoke very little about my parents—and never about that night. If I said anything about my father or mother, they would change the subject, until the whole ordeal became little more than a recurring nightmare. But when I was old enough, I figured out where the house was—the Garrick house—surprised to find it in the same town where my family vacationed every summer. I knew what had happened and still I couldn't stop myself from coming back. I begged my grandparents to let me live here, wanting to be close to it, feeling like it held some part of me. And I learned pretty quickly that people considered it haunted." Nadine sighs, though she manages to retain her composure. "I knew that had to be my mother. I bought the house so I could find a way to set her spirit free."

"I've seen your car driving away both nights I've been there," Brielle says.

"That's because I'm stuck." Nadine sits broken in the chair, her shoulders rounded, back hunched, looking like a remorseful thief begging for forgiveness. There is no more strength to her posture, just an invisible weight she carries. "I go there every night. I know she appears in the window at the same time. She's right there. I can see her looking the way she did the day she died. She stares down at me, asking for help, perhaps knowing that I *know* what happened to her, and yet I can never bring myself to go in. Every night I get there and I'm just that scared little girl again, hiding in the car. Watching as her mother dies."

Her eyes become glassy. And as if she can tell that Brielle notices, Nadine turns her face away. "As soon as it's over I feel the same guilt for having come and not done anything to help her—even though I know she's already dead. Each night I feel more and more sadness piled on me. Like—like bricks stacking up. And even though I never go in, I can't stop going. I just can't. I always think, 'Tonight will be the night that I save her.'"

Brielle moves over so that she's as close to Nadine's armchair as she can be from the couch. She reaches out a hand and places it delicately on the woman's knee, knowing the gesture is not much, but it's all she can think to offer right now. That and her silent presence. She has places she'd rather go—her mind is alight with everything Nadine has just told her, and she wants to return to the Garrick house. But there are moments for action and there are moments to address our pain or the pain of those around us.

This moment belongs to Nadine.

SUBTLE SHADES OF SILENCE

Brielle knows she has only a few hours left before the ghosts disappear for the night, so she wastes little time when she returns to the Garrick house. She drives through the gate and up the overgrown driveway much faster than normal, and even skids on the gravel as she comes to a halt. No sooner does she kill the engine than she's out into the chilly evening air, the breeze blowing loose strands of hair across her face.

Once inside, she lets the front door slam behind her, resounding through the house.

"Aren't we in a hurry," says Parrish from the living room. She spies him slouched on the sofa staring listlessly up at the ceiling, in the same dour mood as always.

"I need to see Laurel."

Parrish raises an eyebrow at her clipped tone. "He's gone, peach. You're too late."

Brielle lets out a frustrated huff. She knew that would be the case, given how late it already is. All the ludicrous rules about time in this house! If anything, they're the reason she can't get the investigation done in a timely manner. Ghosts appearing and disappearing, doors sometimes impassable, as if the house is actively impeding her progress. Or maybe guiding it along at its desired pace—one which clashes directly with hers.

"Of course he is," she mutters.

"We can't help it."

Brielle stares down at the man lying on the couch, knowing he's right and still aggravated by his tone. She has information now. She has a direction. She wants answers. But those answers can't be unearthed without cooperation from the house. Lifting a fist, she kneads her forehead.

"Alright," she says. "That's fine. I can wait to speak with him. I can…"

Her voice drifts. There is one other place she can go.

Leaving Parrish to sulk, she drifts back into the hallway. At the end, the curved staircase leads up toward the floor above. Though it's clean now, she hasn't forgotten the way it looked in the darkness with scarlet blood dripping through the center like rain. She knows eventually the implications of that will come into play, but for now, all that matters is uncovering as much of the story as she can.

The steps mark her progress with soft creaks, following her up onto the landing. Brielle keeps her eyes trained on the stairwell's ceiling, wondering from how high the rain of blood had been falling. But there are no signs that she can see—no further stains. The chandelier hangs unmarked and there's nothing but aging paint and signs of mold in the upper corners.

Continuing to scan the ceiling, Brielle moves into the hallway, knowing that what she's looking for will most likely be up above.

And she's right.

Halfway along the corridor is a thin black rectangle cut into the ceiling. The hallway lights are just dim enough that the door could go unnoticed, but now that she's looking for it, the attic entry feels obvious. Brielle grabs the hooked staff from the corner and raises it up to the door. On one end, a small ring hangs down. She hooks the ring and pulls.

A loud, metallic creak fills the hallway, satisfying in the way it fits into her mental puzzle of this place.

The door opens on rusty springs and comes to rest at a steep incline. Brielle uses the hook again, this time to pull down the folded ladder resting atop the door. It descends into the hallway like the gangly leg of some giant insect and touches neatly against the floor.

Brielle stares up into the black opening. A lightless rectangle where the door had been. She can see absolutely nothing from this vantage point, but wonders if she imagines the icy draft emanating from the blank portal. Is this where the woman in the window hides? Is this from where Rizette and Parrish's sense of dread emanates?

She can't tell without entering.

Brielle steps up onto the first rung, feeling the wood give slightly beneath her weight. She grabs to the ladder with both hands and scans the corridor one last time before beginning her ascent. The climb is not so long—the ceilings are probably twelve feet at most—but each step is somehow monumental. Disjointed, the attic feels as though she'll be entering another world entirely, carried back through the decades by a simple ascension to a realm she hasn't known.

At the top, Brielle slides her phone out of her pocket. She turns on the flashlight and makes a sweep of her surroundings. The attic is large enough that she can't see much save for the underside of the roof to her right and the odd support column here and there. The air has a stagnant stench, not an ugly odor by any means but unpleasant still. Dust hangs in the air, floating in the beam of her light. Knowing she won't be getting anywhere standing in place, Brielle pulls herself the rest of the way in.

As it has always done, the house adjusts around her. Sighing, as if to say, *Ahh, there you are.* But now the space is so confined that it feels like giant hands closing around her instead of watchful eyes. According to the newspaper photograph, there had once been light in this attic, but Brielle cannot find a switch or hanging chain no matter where she looks. Using the light from her phone, she moves in one direction, ducking beneath beams that support the slanted roof until she sees curtains against the wall.

Brielle pulls them wide, revealing the third-floor window. It's small compared to all the others, and round. This late at night, it isn't extraordinarily helpful, but some of the silvery light of the moon finds its way inside. There's a little less darkness around her.

"Salma?" Brielle asks cautiously, facing the attic. She's hopeful for a reply but doesn't believe Salma is the type of ghost who lingers like those below her. She is of a single mind, searching for one thing. And her existence on this plane is rigid and repetitious. An unending cycle that she may not even be aware of.

"Salma?" Brielle asks again, and the silence answers.

But the ghost must be up here in some form. How else would she descend every night? Something in this room *must* tether her.

Brielle continues along the wall, guiding herself by the flashlight. Her circle of illumination reveals aging boards, dust, and cobwebs. A part of the house that had never been given much thought except to exist out of necessity. The roof angles down once more on the other side of the attic, coming to a point with the floorboards, and she tilts her head to the side while she walks. It's much colder up here than in the rest of the house, and she wonders if the floors below have been insulated by a previous owner.

Perhaps there is nothing worth finding up here after all. It's nothing but an empty attic where Salma's spirit takes refuge because it is dark, enclosed, and isolated.

Then Brielle's light falls across a suitcase.

She halts, beam lingering on her discovery. The suitcase is made of worn blue leather, aged over decades sitting in the musty, cold air. A metal handle hangs rusted and dull from the side closest to her, with matching clasps to keep it closed. Judging by the way the large sides bulge ever so slightly, it's been over-packed.

"Salma," Brielle whispers, hoping she's right.

She drops to her knees beside the suitcase, keeping the light trained on it. Her heart pounds purposefully, though it retains a steady rhythm. Leaning forward, she reaches out a hand and—with surprisingly little difficulty—flips open the clasps. As she'd guessed, the suitcase is poorly packed and pops open as soon as it's able, sending a shower of dust racing up into the beam.

Brielle opens it the rest of the way until it's lying flat on the attic floor.

The entire suitcase is full of women's clothing. Blouses and skirts and pants. Undergarments and socks and a coat—colorful, floral patterns typical of the styles worn during Brielle's adolescence. She's hesitant to touch them, knowing that they've sat undisturbed for almost as long as she's been alive. She has to assume they belong to Salma, though it's hard to tell given the spirit's fleeting appearances. Everything has been hastily packed, jumbled and shoved inside as if done in a hurry, with little attention paid to neatness. Brielle pulls a rose blouse loose, holding it up in the light.

The frills on the sleeves are a relic from a different time. They elicit a nostalgia she's not prepared to feel. Setting the blouse down, she reaches inside again.

And her hand brushes against paper.

Brielle frowns, pulling out an envelope.

What had once probably been white has been dyed sepia by time. The paper is fragile and dry, crinkling at the touch of her hand. She flips it over and aims the light.

Rhonda Hartzler
228 Falvey Street
Bangor, ME 04401

Brielle takes a picture of the address, then flips the envelope back over. It's been opened. There are tears in several places along the envelope and flap. The work of over-eager hands—perhaps someone who didn't care whether or not they were the intended recipient.

Lifting the flap, Brielle pulls a single sheet of folded paper from inside. It's just as dried and fragile as the envelope. Lined as if it was torn straight out of a notebook. She unfolds the sheet, revealing neat, narrow writing scrawled across the page in black ink. Simply a poem with no other message.

> *I'll find you as the autumn turns to drear*
> *And sunlight dies upon the lurid scape*
> *Amid this all, my heart will bloom sincere*
> *For in your likeness love will take its shape*
> *While harbors and the rivers, streams, and lakes*
> *Freeze over in the falling of new snow*
> *A comfort in spring promises I take*
> *Once buried, then in death do flowers grow*
> *I loathe my dreams for leaving me to wake*

From knowing how it feels with you beside
But in the fate foretold by dreams I take
Some solace knowing soon you will arrive
From then, we'll chase the moon through skies above
The nature of an unrestricted love

Brielle reads the poem again. And when she's finished, a third time. She flips the sheet over, but nothing else has been written. All that was inside the envelope is this poem. Carefully, she folds it back up, sliding it into the envelope once more. When this is done, she places it back into the suitcase, which she closes as well, leaving nothing to suggest that she's been here at all. A sadness has overcome her. It emanates from the note, despite the words of love written there. Despite the hopeful message scrawled across the page. Brielle can feel this sadness weighing on her heart, and she finds she no longer wishes to be here in the attic. This is wrong.

This is all wrong.

The floor creaks.

Brielle lifts her phone, shining her light into the darkness. The sound had come from somewhere near the ladder. Loud and pointed, as if something had applied its weight over there.

"Salma?" she asks, but there is no reply. Only a heavy, oppressive silence.

Standing as much as she can beneath the slanted ceiling, she takes one step toward the open door. As she does so, the floorboards creak beneath her.

And again from the opposite corner of the room.

Brielle freezes, holding her breath. She strains her eyes against the inadequate light, her ears ringing to discern between the different shades of silence. Moonlight continues to waft into the room from the window, but it's not enough to illuminate the dark corner.

Not taking her eyes off the shadows, Brielle takes another cautious step forward. The house shifts to accommodate her, marking her movements as it does everywhere she goes. One step, then another, slowly making her way to the exit.

Creeeeeeak.

Brielle's eyes are wide. The attic around her stays empty. Still, she can feel something else with her now. Is it her imagination hiding in the dark corner unseen? With every step the additional noise sounds, signaling the movement of the other. It keeps pace with her, stalking her. It doesn't like what she found. She wasn't supposed to open the suitcase. Find the envelope. Read the note.

She wasn't supposed to know.

At the top of the ladder, Brielle clenches her teeth. She can't hold on with both hands and continue to aim the light. She'll need to descend one-handed. Lowering her foot onto the first rung, she sweeps the light across the corner where the other waits. Resolute shadows stare back. Nothing. No angry spirits. She's letting the house get to her. How rarely this happens. Why is she letting it have such an effect?

Creeeeeeeak.

Brielle pauses, light aimed directly at the source. There's no doubting the other is there, their movements as audible as any of her own. The light is blinding and yet inadequate as ever. Dissipated by the incessant blizzard of floating dust particles. Where it should cut through, there is only black.

Black and the silvery moon from the curtains she hasn't closed.

But that will be for another time. She can come back tomorrow if she needs to—when the daylight is far more helpful.

She lowers her other foot to the next rung.

And the shadows move.

Panicked, Brielle nearly loses her hold on the ladder, hastening to descend. Her heart hammers in her chest, mind blank. Every instinct tells her to get away as quickly as possible. No time to register what emerged from the darkness. She flings her arms against the steps, not bothering to watch where she's going. The beam of the flashlight sweeps wildly across the ceiling. She stares up into the darkness, hoping whatever had moved doesn't appear above her.

Halfway down, she misses a rung. Her foot sinks through the air. Her hand slips off the ladder, flailing wildly through the air, looking for purchase. There's a loud crack as the rung beneath her other foot snaps and then she's falling. She doesn't have time to scream before the floor rushes up to meet her and the air is knocked from her lungs. Everything around her flickers out of focus for a moment, dissolving into white. But she demands her consciousness remain.

Vision swimming, a pained groan escaping her lips, Brielle searches for the hooked staff. She finds it on the ground beside her, then rolls up onto her knees.

Is the shadow following her? Is it coming? Or does it watch her from above, satisfied that she's left the attic?

Brielle doesn't want to find out. She folds the ladder up, the springs helping to alleviate the weight. Then she hooks the ring and with a harried shove closes the attic door. It wails in protest as per usual but doesn't fight her, and as it slams closed, dust and dislodged bits of plaster rain down.

The debris lands in her hair, and Brielle stands in the dark hallway, panting. For several minutes, she does nothing, waiting for her pulse to slow. It usually takes a lot to frighten her—certainly more than movements in the shadows—but something about the air in that attic, the cadence of the house, the emotions she felt emanating in that space, overwhelmed her. And now, she doesn't know what to make of her experience.

Could that have been the presence of Salma Toren? Was that the form she takes while hiding up above? Brielle can't rule out the possibility, though it seems wrong. That's not the typical aura of a fleeting ghost.

When she finally gathers her composure, Brielle replaces the hooked staff in the corner. Glancing back up at the attic door, which remains quiet and closed, she descends to the first floor. It'll reopen before the end of the night. Hopefully she won't be around when it does.

For now, she has a new piece of the puzzle to investigate— the existence of a Rhonda Hartzler. Brielle might've taken her to be one of the admirers Laurel had mentioned during their conversation, except that the poem was addressed *to* Rhonda. Thinking of the poem causes another surge of sadness. The passion it conveyed, the desperation in the face of repressed feelings. There could be no misconstruing. Salma had loved Rhonda—or at least, she thought she did. Was there much of a difference? Brielle will have to know more before she can answer that.

NUMBER THE HAUNTED

"You're leaving again?"

She stops feet from the front door. Light shines through the entrance to the living room, and she sees Parrish still slumped on the couch. He has his feet on the coffee table, his fingers interlaced across his stomach as he stares up at the ceiling. The lamp beside him glows amber.

"Yes, there's really no use in me staying," Brielle says. "What with all of you disappearing every night."

"Not"—he clicks his tongue—"all of us."

"Yes, well, she's not a great conversationalist."

Parrish nods. "I don't blame you. I would leave too if I could. That'll be the first thing I do once you free us."

"You might not have much of a choice," Brielle says, smiling.

"My bag has been packed for decades," Parrish says. He grabs the edge of the seat beneath him and hoists himself so that he's sitting upright. "So there won't be anything holding me back, babes. I'll just—"

He makes a *whooshing* sound. Brielle chuckles, trying not to let on that she's still preoccupied by what happened upstairs.

"No holds barred."

He sits back, obviously dwelling on the thought. "Do you know what comes next?"

Brielle doesn't answer right away. She searches her mental catalog of all the jobs she's taken—all the ones of note, at least. Every spirit she encountered. The ones in denial, the corporeal ones, the abstract ones, the strong and the weak. And the vitriolic. She answers with complete certainty.

"No," she says. "I have absolutely no idea what comes next. By the time anyone I've helped finds out, I've lost all contact."

"Pity," Parrish says. "You don't even know where you're sending us."

"My suspicion is that I'm not sending you anywhere."

He nods again.

"Does that scare you?" Brielle asks.

"It used to," Parrish says. "But repetition is only useful if it ends eventually."

Brielle lowers herself into one of the armchairs. The glow of the lamp washes over her, dyeing her clothes amber. But she accepts the light's warmth. It's welcoming, like a beacon to somewhere safe, a reprieve from the blues and blacks and browns of the house. As she sits, she glances toward the bay window. Remnants of the image of Salma's ghost standing there linger in her mind.

"I wasn't good when I was alive," Parrish says.

"In what way?"

He hangs his head. "I killed my brother."

Can he mean that literally? While Brielle admits she hasn't spent much time with the man, she hadn't judged him to be the type to murder anyone. Not that there is one type of killer, but most have some common traits.

"How?" she asks.

"Neglect."

"Were you—"

"He wasn't right in the head," Parrish says, combing his hair back with one hand. "He had a lot of mental issues. And sometimes he was fine—I mean, he lived by himself. So he could function alright. But I didn't know—I couldn't know how to handle his issues. He was always calling me. Always."

The spirit turns his head, looking into Brielle's eyes. His casual nonchalance is gone, that breezy demeanor he'd kept up since her arrival. For the first time, she can see desperation in him. Guilt.

"I couldn't deal with my own shit. I couldn't have my own life because I'd have a girl in my room and—and suddenly he'd be calling me. Crying his eyes out because he was too anxious to go to the grocery store or something like that. And I was the *only* one he would call. The only one. Not our parents, not the doctors I introduced him to. He didn't have any other friends because he didn't want to talk to somebody else. It was always me." Parrish stabs himself in the chest with both thumbs, pleading with Brielle to understand the position he was in.

"So one night he calls me. I had a real nice lady over at my house for dinner. Tonya Cole. She liked me a lot, I could tell, and I sure as hell liked her too. We're laughing it up, making eyes at each other. I'm thinking that I might have a second date with her on the horizon and maybe some sex tonight, and my phone starts ringing. I don't answer it. This is the one I don't want to get away. The connection I've been looking for. Why should I sacrifice that? He calls again—*incessantly*. Because that's what he does. Tonya's asking me who's trying to get ahold of me so bad and why I won't just pick up. But I'd been through this a hundred times already. A lady doesn't like to be ignored. Especially on a first date. Nobody does.

"She's a little weirded out, so she goes to the bathroom. While she's in there, I answer." Parrish has run his hand through his hair a dozen times now, though every time it falls right back into place. "Merv is on the other end, of course. He says, all pathetic, 'Parrish, I need you.' And I was so angry. I was so tired of having my life interrupted all the time by him. I practically screamed. I said, 'Leave me alone.' And I hung up."

The sound of the phone slamming down on the receiver echoes through the room. The finality of it, the implications of his angry statement. Parrish even stands, his hand outstretched as if reaching to pick it up again. If he's fast enough, maybe the call won't have dropped yet. Merv will still be waiting on the other end of the line.

"He was found dead the next day. Knife in his hand and blood on the floor." Almost as if he doesn't realize he's moving, Parrish steps around the coffee table. He stares momentarily at the darkness through the window, then turns away, clenching and unclenching his fists. His voice is weak and hoarse. "It was my fault. It was because of me, because I didn't pick up and sit and talk him down. I let him die."

"You didn't know," Brielle says, standing too.

"But I did." Parrish smiles ruefully. "I just wanted it to stop."

He stares down at his hands as if they are covered in something Brielle can't see. The blood of his brother, maybe.

"It stopped alright. But all that came of it was numbness," he whispers. "From the moment he was found, everything was numb. Telling my parents. The funeral. Everything that followed after was so incredibly empty. For so long I had wanted him to stop shedding his pain on me, and once he died, there was nothing left to feel."

"Did he live here?" Brielle asks, thinking that maybe this is what brought Parrish to the Garrick house.

"In Camden? No," Parrish says, shaking his head. "No, this was me trying to escape. After so much numbness, I started searching for pain. I didn't know how to—how to *cope* without it. I didn't deserve to feel anything else, did I? Not after what I'd done. After how I'd let him and our family down." The floorboards creak as Parrish wanders out of the living room. The house sighs, breathing comfort toward him. "I took to drink and cutting."

Brielle follows him. Even in the dark she can see his bare forearms. They're clean. Smooth, unblemished skin. Perhaps he notices her questioning looks.

"I didn't cut where my brother cut that night," Parrish explains softly. "I didn't want anybody to know. I didn't want anyone trying to comfort me with pitying words about how I couldn't really be to blame. 'He'd done it to himself, that couldn't be helped.' I cut the insides of my thighs. The easiest way to feel pain."

"I'm so sorry," Brielle says, though her words feel woefully inadequate.

"I am too," Parrish replies. He stops at the open door to the bathroom. The inside is nearly pitch black, with only the faintest visible outline of the things inside—the sink and vanity, the tub, the toilet. He stares in, chin jutting forward, his hands gripping the doorframe as if holding to an anchor to keep from being washed away. "It was never enough. None of it. But it was the only thing that felt right, so I kept doing it. Over and over. Eager to see that satisfying line of blood seeping out of me.

"When I grew tired of my parents hounding me to come over every damn night as if I could cure their sadness, I left. I came here, thinking that there was nobody who could bother me in Camden, Maine.

"I was right."

Brielle almost tries to put her hand on his shoulder, wanting to comfort him, but remembers at the last moment that her hand will only pass right through. She can't help him this way. She can't help any of them this way. She can only bring them peace through resolution.

"Parrish," she says. "You didn't do this to yourself."

He doesn't look at her, but he does turn his head away from the sight of the bathroom.

"You were murdered. You and Rizette." She almost mentions Salma, but she doesn't think he knows her name.

"By who?" he asks.

"I don't know. Not for certain, anyways, but I think it was Laurel. The evidence suggests—"

"I don't remember," Parrish says, and turns away again. "He might have. I couldn't tell you, but I don't think it matters."

"How can you say that?"

From down the hall, she hears a door snap closed—the office closet. Time is running short. Parrish releases his hold on the doorframe and steps into the darkened bathroom. "Even if he hadn't killed me," he says, "I would've died in this house anyway."

The door swings slowly shut behind him and Brielle is suddenly plunged into darkness.

And from the living room, she hears the clock strike half past nine. Knowing what's to come, Brielle departs. Just as she slides through the front door, she hears the metallic creak of the attic opening.

The door closes of its own accord.

Brielle turns away from the house, facing the stairs that lead down to her car. But as she gazes out at the circular driveway, her heart sinks through her stomach. Something is not right. The top of her car reflects the moonlight, but a misshapen mass lies across the hood. She removes her phone from her pocket again, but she's too far away for the flashlight to reveal whatever's waiting for her. Her teeth clench, muscles tensed, ready to run should the situation call for it. But whatever waits for her is immobile.

The wind changes direction and Brielle catches the stench of decay. She covers her mouth and nose, squinting against the dark, inching ever closer to her car while her mind pleads for her to look away.

But she can't go anywhere without her car. She can't get to her motel or the soft, safe bed waiting for her there. She will not strand herself here for another night.

Another step, and now she can make out spindly, twisted limbs. Fur-covered skin marred by darkened lacerations. Black flies hover about it, picking at the rotting flesh. And as she moves around the car toward the driver's side—leaving a wide berth between her and the carcass—the flashlight comes across the staring, lifeless head of a deer.

Brielle spins on the spot, the light tracing the wild edge of the driveway. Her pulse thrums in her ears, her breath billowing out of her mouth in a silvery mist. The trees and the tall weeds sway in the wind, their dark forms ominous and hulking in the night. She sees nothing else and yet she has never felt so watched.

But the night isn't over.

A car comes whipping up the road without its headlights on. Brielle turns, heart leaping into her throat. But as it comes to a stop, anger and fear flood through her and she storms over to the new arrival.

Nadine opens her window but doesn't get out. "Brielle?"

"Did you do this?" Brielle asks, trying to keep her voice from shaking. "Was this you?"

"What are you talking about?"

"My car!" Brielle shouts, pointing at the dead deer on the hood of her Volkswagen.

"I just got here—"

"You could've come back, made it look like you're innocent! *Did you or didn't you?*"

"No, Brielle! Why would I? I'm the one who hired you to be here." Nadine still hasn't gotten out of the car, but she raises her hands in surrender, a silent plea for Brielle to calm down.

But Brielle doesn't want to calm down. Not after this. Not after the evening she's had—crawling through the attic, being chased, and now a rotting carcass left for her to find. There may be four spirits haunting that house and waiting for release, but this case has far exceeded what she'd come here expecting. She doesn't like this latest turn.

"Then why are you late?" she asks, still suspicious, though she lowers her voice. "You're here every night, but tonight you're late. Why?"

Nadine lowers her gaze, sighing with disappointment. "I tried to stay away," she says. "After our conversation, I wanted to break free of the cycle."

Brielle doesn't know how to respond. Her anger continues to ebb, though her senses remain elevated.

"I failed," Nadine finishes. "I couldn't stay away."

When she looks back up, it's like a child expecting punishment. And Brielle realizes that while she might be able to move about wherever she pleases, Nadine is just as trapped as any of the spirits inside the house. She wants them freed just as much as she wants her own freedom, even if she doesn't realize it.

Brielle was wrong. There are five souls trapped in the Garrick house.

A HOUSE IN BANGOR

Sleep is hard to find that night, which is often the case at this point in a job. Between her discussions with Nadine, the trip to the attic, Parrish's confession, and the deer carcass, Brielle cannot find the space to quiet her mind. The minutes melt into hours marked only by her changes in position.

It doesn't help that Brielle looked up the address on the envelope for Rhonda, and the woman lives only an hour and a half away. It now seems that, contrary to Laurel's beliefs—or ignorance, or denial—Salma had been the one doing the admiring. Why were her belongings in the attic anyway? Would this Rhonda have any answers? Brielle wants to leave and drive up to Bangor. She isn't the least bit tired, so there isn't any danger in it being too late. But she reasons that even if she leaves now, Rhonda isn't likely to be awake. And a stranger at the door at 2 a.m. isn't likely to get someone to open up.

No, lying in bed repeating an endless cycle of useless thoughts proves more annoying than helpful. By the time sleep does find her, it's late enough that Brielle spends most of the morning with her head under her pillow. The inadequate curtains on the window let too much light in, but she's so tired that she doesn't let it rouse her until the clock reads nearly eleven. Then she finally drags herself out of her warm cocoon and into the shower.

She dresses, brushes her teeth, and grabs a granola bar from the paper bag of groceries sitting atop the dresser. Then she's out the door.

Despite the persistent chill in the air, bright rays of sun stream through the cloud cover, appearing like brief, angelic spotlights before going dim again and appearing elsewhere. Her car sits beneath an angled awning. She'd gone to a gas station on the way back to the motel last night, to scrub the hood with the complementary windshield squeegee. Surprisingly, there hadn't been much blood, despite the stench of the corpse. In the daylight, she searches for anything she might have missed, but the hood appears clean.

While she waits for the engine to warm up, spewing white puffs of heavy vapor into the air behind her, she eats the granola bar in silence. The radio isn't tuned to any station, and she hasn't initiated her phone's GPS so it isn't barking directions at her. There's just the gentle rumble of the car and the sticky maple-and-walnut morsels in her mouth. In this moment, part of her doubts the nutrition information on the box. How can something so sweet be considered healthy? It tastes less like the bars she's used to eating and more like the donuts her mother used to buy her and her brother on the way to school some random mornings when her cravings overtook her willpower. Brielle remembers the miniscule shop in the strip mall beside the grocery store—barely large enough to fit a group of four inside. The glass case sat right up against the front window, offering a spread of sweet, fluffy delectables, each more alluring than the last. Kam was partial to the chocolate rings, as was their mother. But Brielle? No, she went for the maple bars. She always felt clever for having picked the largest donut. Mom swore the rings were the same size, but how could that be true when the maple bar had such a wide, uninterrupted surface of golden goodness?

They'd sit in the car, the three of them. Eating their breakfast treats as though sharing in a naughty secret. Giggling conspiratorially before Mom cleaned them up and took them the rest of the way to school.

She never knew when donut days would come. The surprise was part of the fun. Those were the best of times. Pure, untainted moments of happiness.

~

The drive to Bangor goes quickly. Brielle turns the radio to a station playing bland pop-rock hits that slide by as seamlessly as the miles of highway. She follows the instructions on her phone almost without hearing them, used to driving distances without much thought. Her mind is elsewhere, though she can't pinpoint its coordinates. Just not here, in this car, on Highway 1 with a bleak but grassy Maine beyond the windows.

By the time Falvey Street sneaks up on her, Brielle is almost surprised.

The homes are modest rectangular boxes sitting back from the road amid barren trees and cut grass. Not one is too dissimilar from the next, though their colors are different enough to distinguish them. Sidewalks made of the same asphalt as the road connect the homes like strings of Christmas lights. The properties are not separated; there are no fences. And the only streetlamps

Brielle can see are set high on the telephone poles that run along one side of the street.

She parks outside number 228, wishing there had been a phone number to call to announce her arrival. She hasn't seen a single person out and about, though there is a well-traveled Honda Civic parked in the gravel driveway.

Brielle takes a deep breath and approaches the front door, aware of how out of place she looks in this neighborhood where she guesses everyone knows one another. There's no doorbell, so she opens the screen door and knocks.

"Hello?" she says, and clears her throat after hearing the waver in her voice.

To her relief, footsteps sound from inside.

Sheer curtains are drawn over the front window, but Brielle spies a shadow moving across the room. A few seconds later the door opens to reveal a squat woman with a gray bob and narrow, suspicious eyes. She has on a navy cardigan which dangles loose from her ample bosom. Around her neck hangs a pair of gold-rimmed glasses.

"And who might you be?" the woman asks.

"Brielle Panya. I'm looking for Rhonda Hartzler."

The woman narrows her eyes further, assessing whether or not she wants to answer. Brielle doesn't know what she's done to deserve this treatment, but she continues to stand awkwardly on the doorstep.

"I'm sorry to tell you I'm not her," the woman says finally. "She doesn't live here anymore."

Brielle's heart sinks. Damn. Of course Rhonda doesn't live in this house anymore—it's been nearly thirty years.

"Do you know where she is now?" Brielle asks, hoping this woman can at least point her in the right direction. Without any other means of finding Rhonda, this lead could easily slip away.

"Why do you want to know?"

This is the moment where Brielle has to determine how much of the truth she wants to reveal. If she outright lies, her story must be convincing enough to persuade this already suspicious woman to help her. If she tells the truth and this woman doesn't believe in the supernatural, then she'll almost certainly be dismissed without a second thought. Brielle glances past the woman into the house. Visible behind her is a small corner of her living room—pale pink walls, a worn couch, and a hanging cross.

"I'm investigating someone's death."

"Are you a reporter?"

"No. More like a private investigator," Brielle says, which is not untruthful. "I have reason to believe that Rhonda and the subject of my investigation may have been involved. Romantically."

Brielle's statement has an unmistakable effect on the woman. Her frown softens and she stands up straighter, though her posture—positioned at any time to slam the door in Brielle's face— doesn't change.

"Oh," she says in a quiet voice.

Seizing upon a hunch, Brielle goes further. "The person whose death I'm investigating was named Salma Toren."

"Oh," the woman says again, and this time she backs away from the door. "Why don't you come inside."

Glad to no longer be on display, Brielle follows the woman indoors. The interior of the house is warm, almost stiflingly so. She enters the living room, and the woman gestures for her to take a seat on the couch. Brielle does so, taking stock of the many blankets and pillows strewn across the furniture. Across from her, a small flat-screen TV sits on a black entertainment stand, a muted gameshow playing out in silence. Framed photographs seem to occupy the rest of the surfaces, covering the end tables, the coffee table, and a few shelves on the walls.

"Tea? Coffee?" the woman asks from another room.

"Tea, please," Brielle says, realizing she hadn't had anything to drink with her breakfast.

"It'll be ready in a moment," the woman says, returning and taking her seat in a quilted rocking chair. She crosses her arms as her descent into the chair sends her backward. "Salma Toren," she muses. "That's a name I haven't heard in a long time. What did you say yours was again?"

"Brielle."

"That's got a nice ring to it. Uncommon."

"My parents heard it on a talk show while they were pregnant with me."

The woman nods as if this makes sense to her. "Mine is Miranda."

"And you know Rhonda?"

"Knew, I'm afraid."

Brielle's heart sinks a little further. "Oh, I'm sorry to hear that. I didn't know."

"S'alright. Happened about five years ago now."

"Did you know her well?"

"I should hope so," Miranda says with a smirk. "She was my wife."

Suddenly, Brielle realizes that more than a few of the photographs arranged around the room are of the same woman with black, wavy hair and a wide smile. In fact, the more she looks, Brielle finds photographs of this woman from nearly every stage of life—young and lithe lying out on a dock in a lake, made up and poised in a smart-looking dress, even a few where signs of wrinkles have begun to show themselves around her identifying smile.

"Is that her?" Brielle asks, gesturing to one of these photographs.

Miranda nods. "That's my Rhonda."

"She's beautiful."

"You're telling me." Miranda chuckles.

"How long were you married?"

"That depends," she says with a raised eyebrow. "Technically we were only married for four years, once it became legal here in Maine, but in my mind, it was more like twenty. From the moment she asked me to move in with her."

"That must've been wonderful," Brielle says, "to have been with someone for so long."

"She was the light in any room. The life of the party. The type of person people thought of at random times in their day. 'I was at the park and I saw these great egrets, Rhonda. And I thought of how much you like birds.' That sort of thing," she says, rocking gently in her chair. "Rhonda was enthusiastic about all sorts of topics, you see. And it was all genuine. You could be into rocks or something. One conversation with her and she'd make you feel like you had the most interesting hobby in the world."

"She couldn't have been *that* perfect," Brielle says before she can stop herself.

"I can assure you she was," Miranda retorts.

"I'm always impressed by people with that kind of social stamina," Brielle says, hoping she hasn't accidentally erased the woman's good will toward her. To her relief, this doesn't seem to be the case.

"I couldn't care less about half the shit people say," Miranda says, laughing. "But she did. Made me all the better for it, possibly. All I know is, once she was gone, more than half the people fell out of touch with me."

Brielle doesn't know what to say, even if Miranda apparently finds this detail hilarious.

"S'alright. It was all her, I'll admit it. I didn't give a damn about most of them anyway."

"If you don't mind me asking," Brielle says, "what happened to her?"

"Bad heart," Miranda says gruffly. "God has a wicked sense of humor, doesn't he?"

She lifts herself out of the chair and pads off toward the kitchen to fetch their tea, shaking her head along the way as if still confounded by the matter. Brielle stares down at the closest image of Rhonda, thinking that if she believed in God she might agree. The truth was, she didn't think anything out there was in control. At least, not anything that cared about what a person did when they were alive. It's only from the people around them that anyone receives justice in life.

And what little of that there is to go around.

Miranda returns with two steaming mugs in her hands.

"I decided we're having black tea," she says. "I hope that's fine with you. Oh, and milk—and sugar. Easier to make two of the same thing."

"Perfect," Brielle says, doubtful that the woman would've remade it had she declined. Her host gestures to a stack of coasters, so Brielle takes one before setting her mug down on the coffee table.

"Her passing was quick," Miranda says, delving straight back into their conversation as she stares into the steam rising from her mug. "One day she was here and the next…gone."

"That must've been a difficult change for you."

Miranda shifts, setting down her mug a bit harder than is necessary. She crosses her arms over her chest again, and Brielle gets the idea that this is not a woman used to acknowledging her emotions. In fact, she seems almost flustered by a statement that Brielle would consider relatively innocuous.

"It wasn't a walk in the park, I can tell you that." She brushes a strand of hair away from her eyes. "But you aren't here to ask me about Rhonda."

I suppose I wasn't. But now that I know Rhonda is dead, how will I break the cycle of hauntings?

"Rhonda told you about Salma?"

"Of course—in a healthy relationship, you end up learning everything," Miranda says. Now that the conversation has been successfully redirected, she picks up her tea again. "Besides which, why shouldn't I know? It was before I came along."

"What exactly did she say?"

"Well, it wasn't a happy story, I'll tell you that." Miranda takes a sip. On the end table beside her, there's a framed photograph of Rhonda with a trio of children posing together in a park. "She was always a good cook—had an excellent instinct for mixing flavors. Before she bought this house, she lived in Portland and worked as the head chef in an Italian restaurant.

"That's where they met. She and Salma. They ran into each other outside the bathroom one day and…I suppose they were both smitten. Enough so that Salma frequented the restaurant almost weekly. Only she was married," Miranda says with a grim smile. "To a man. Things were a lot harder back then—still are for some. The pressure to control your *deviance*, the pressure to just go along with how things were supposed to be and hope with all your goddamn might that you'd eventually love him, was inescapable for most. For a select few, there was hope of acceptance, but that was rare."

Miranda sets down the mug again and raises her hands as if warding away the thoughts. "Of course, as soon as they fell for each other, Salma regretted marrying her husband. You didn't expect to find a happy relationship back then. If anything, it was secretive flings unless you were lucky. Unless you cut most everyone else out of your life. Everyone but the other folk like you.

"But they started writing letters to each other. Rhonda didn't have anyone at the time, so she could write freely, but Salma had to be careful that nobody find out. From the way Rhonda told it, it wasn't that she didn't like her husband. He was fine enough, but she didn't love him. Not in that way. And she didn't think he was the type to understand. He was the traditional sort—a good ol' Christian boy, worked an office job, wanted kids. That wasn't Salma, try as she might. She didn't want any of those things. She wanted Rhonda, and Rhonda wanted her.

"So eventually, they made a plan to be together. Rhonda bought this house, and when the time was right, they agreed to meet halfway between here and Portland. Salma knew of an inn somewhere, I guess. She would ditch her car there so she couldn't be found and Rhonda would take her the rest of the way. Then they'd have a new life here in good old Bangor. A life together away from all the expectations."

Brielle realizes she hasn't had any of her tea yet. She lifts the mug to her lips as Miranda sighs and wipes the eyeglasses she hasn't been wearing with her shirt.

"Did things not go to plan?" Brielle prompts when the woman doesn't continue.

"No. No, not at all," Miranda says darkly. "Of course, I can only say what Rhonda told me, so I probably don't know all the details—only what was important to her. But the way she told it, she was leaving to get Salma when she got a call from the inn. Salma was there already, talking about how things were better than she could've imagined. About how they wouldn't have to be so secretive after all. Apparently, her husband had known about Rhonda's letters and confronted her. When she explained, he wasn't happy, but he understood that her sexual orientation wasn't a choice and that if she was unhappy, he couldn't stop her from leaving. That went completely against their expectations, but it was the best kind of surprise. Then Salma said the only thing he asked was that she visit her daughter from time to time.

"Rhonda hadn't known about her daughter."

The image of Nadine swims into Brielle's mind. How could something like the existence of a daughter go unmentioned? Especially since it seemed like Rhonda and Salma had been exchanging letters for years. Their bond had been strong enough for Salma to upend her life, to pen such impassioned poetry. Amid all that, she'd never thought to mention her daughter?

"Rhonda drove to the inn," Miranda continues, her words slow, becoming almost reluctant. "She thought about Salma's daughter the whole way there, and when she arrived at the inn, she saw a car parked out front with a little girl waiting in the backseat. That was too much for her. And even though they had longed for each other in secret all this time, she couldn't bring herself to follow through. She left—without going in, without saying anything to

Salma. She drove back here despite her broken heart. But she couldn't do it anymore."

"Rhonda was there at the inn?" Brielle asks, breathless.

Miranda nods. "I know what you're thinking—how could she have given up like that? But you have to understand, Rhonda came from a broken family. Her father had walked out on her when she was young. She never wanted to do that to a child. So you see, she couldn't break up that house. Not when she knew that meant leaving the girl motherless."

"But she was there that night?"

Miranda nods again. "She tried writing to Salma again after leaving, to apologize and explain—called their house too, but there was no response. Not even from the husband. She figured that Salma didn't want anything to do with her anymore. What she'd done was unforgivable even if Rhonda had her reasons.

"It wasn't until years later that she figured out Salma died that night. I was with Rhonda for twenty years," Miranda says. "I can tell you there are few things she regretted more than running out on Salma. Of course, she always reassured me that she never regretted meeting me, but if she hadn't come back so quickly, if she hadn't left Salma there, she'd probably still be alive today."

"Possibly," Brielle says. "But there's no way she could've known."

"That's what I always told her. I don't know if she ever truly believed that. I don't think she ever forgot it either."

"Nothing can hurt you quite like your own mind." Brielle stares down at the photo of Rhonda again. The way she's posed, smiling straight into the camera, she could be looking back at Brielle.

"I have to ask," Miranda says, "why you were hoping to find Rhonda here. What're you looking for?"

"An end to the cycle," Brielle says. "I was hired by Salma's daughter, Nadine. She was the little girl Rhonda saw in the car."

Miranda inhales sharply, her eyes widening. Brielle sets her mug down.

"Haunted houses come in all sorts," she says. "And I do what I can to quiet them."

WHAT HE WANTED

The phone rings twice on the other end, but before Brielle can change her mind and hang up, it's answered.

"Hello?"

"Kam," she says, a little breathless from feeling unprepared. "I…uh, how're you doing?"

"I'm fine, Brielle. How about you?"

"I'll do it," she says.

"What?" He seems confused. He has a right to feel confused. After all, she hadn't known she was going to call until the moment she entered her car.

"I'll speak. At Mom's funeral. I can give a eulogy."

"Are you sure?" he asks. She can hear him rummaging, probably leaving himself a note. "Only if you want to."

"I want to," Brielle says.

After they hang up, she drives the rest of the way in silence. Even the radio feels like too much of a distraction, so she shuts it off. Bangor becomes highway becomes Camden, and before long she's pulling into the driveway of the Garrick Estate. She doesn't take the time to close the gate, reasoning that she doesn't expect to be here for long.

Inside, she finds Rizette emerging from the office.

"Hello," she says, as if expecting a guest. After a moment's hesitation, though, she recognizes Brielle.

"I'm looking for Laurel."

The innkeeper is a little taken aback by Brielle's bluntness. She blinks. "The last I saw he was in the kitchen. You can—"

Brielle mutters a quick thank you before crossing through the living room into the dining area. She doesn't have to search hard for her subject. Laurel is sitting at the table with a book in his hand. The name Mitchell is visible on the cover before he sets it face down and looks up at her.

"I hear you're looking for me," he says with a light grin.

"You lied," Brielle says. She steps up to the chair opposite him and wraps her fingers around the top of the backrest.

"I beg your pardon."

"Don't play games, please. I knew you weren't telling me the truth when we spoke before. I just didn't know about what."

She expects Laurel to be angry, or somewhat peeved by her accusations. At the very least, he will deny her claims, staunchly defending his integrity and how his side of the story is technically true from his point of view. This is often the case of spirits who are unaware that they're holding themselves hostage on this plane of existence. Acknowledging their own fabrications is sometimes enough to cut their tether. But Laurel does nothing that she expects. He folds his hands over the top of his book and looks quietly defeated. Remorseful. Tired.

All of which confirms that he lied with intention.

When he doesn't respond, Brielle continues. "You didn't die with the rest of them, did you? Rizette and Parrish disappear every night at nine thirty when Salma comes, but not you. You vanish by six. I found an article at the library from 1992. There was a triple homicide, and those three were the victims."

At the name of his wife, Laurel flinches—a reaction that doesn't go unnoticed by Brielle. Still, he doesn't look up at her; he stares resolutely at the back of his hands, his mouth a straight line.

"You didn't die with them," she repeats.

"No," he whispers. "I killed myself much later."

"Did you know that your daughter was the one who hired me?"

Surprise in the arch of his eyebrows, the way his lips part.

"She told me that you were the suspected killer."

Eye contact.

"Don't you have anything to say to that?"

She has him. Brielle knows it. He may not be corporeal, but behind his countenance she can tell that there are a thousand thoughts running through his mind, flashes of memories that he has forgotten for perhaps years now. He slumps back in his chair, assaulted by the rush and unable to comprehend it. How does it feel to have a lifetime breathed into you all at once?

"I did," he says slowly. "I—"

"You did what, Laurel?"

His gaze is as distant as his voice, bridging the void of decades. "She was leaving me." He lifts his hands to his face, covering his eyes, trying to block out the images. Trying to steady himself. "She was leaving. She—she received secret letters from her lover for years, but she wasn't always so great about hiding them. I found a few. Of course, they were all from that woman. That *bitch* who invaded our lives. I thought she was an obsessed admirer. The way she would carry on and on about Salma, I thought she was simply deluded. And I never brought it up because I thought surely Salma was just putting up with it. After all, I never saw her respond—not initially, at least. That was my mistake. My naivete. But I should've seen the signs. The glances. The avoidance. Hell, she didn't even love our daughter. But again, I should've seen that coming too. She'd never wanted a child, never expressed any interest until the night we conceived her."

Brielle can see him becoming aggravated—his sentences stilted and disconnected. She needs to bring him back on course if she wants a straight story out of him. "When did you realize the letters weren't just delusions?"

Laurel runs a hand across his forehead. "I came home from work one day and she was out by her car—looked like she'd just closed the trunk. I knew something was happening, but she didn't want to tell me. Kept saying how she just needed to run out real quick for something. It didn't feel right, so I told her I knew about the letters. She changed her tune immediately. Started crying her eyes out. And I felt bad, like I'd done something wrong to her.

"She confessed then and there. Said she...she loved Rhonda. She was a lesbian and couldn't hide it any longer. Despite almost a decade of being together, she didn't love me in that way and realized she never could." He traces lines on the back cover of the book with his finger while he talks, eyes downcast. "I was shocked. Sure, we weren't as close as we used to be, we certainly didn't have sex as often as I would've liked, but I never thought—but that was that. And I could tell by the look in her eye that this was something she'd thought about for a long time. This was something she had no influence over. I had no choice but to believe her despite my prior convictions—even if I wanted to think she was doing it just to be cruel. But that wasn't her. That kind of cruelty wasn't in my Salma."

"What did you do?"

"I didn't know how to react, so I let her go. I was angry, I'll admit. Defeated too. I told her if this was the only way she could be happy then she'd better leave. But God knows, if she was going to walk out of our day-to-day life, she'd still better come to see Nadine. Because that girl was old enough that she wouldn't forget her mom. Not anytime soon.

"I guess some part of me probably thought she'd back down once I said that, but she didn't. She just thanked me and left." Laurel goes quiet, his fingers coming to rest. Brielle knows what must follow. She wants him to say it, but if she pressures him, he might resist. "I went inside and found Nadine in front of the TV. Salma had just left our daughter there. Wasn't even going to wait for me to come home before sneaking off. Sad as I was, I tried not to let it show. Nadine didn't ask any questions. It hadn't registered yet for her. Any minute Mom would be back from the store. We watched a *Cheers* episode together, then ate dinner, just the two of us at the table. But it wasn't until I was getting ready to put her to bed that she asked me, 'Where's Mommy? Isn't she going to kiss me goodnight?'"

Laurel works his jaw in a circle, his heavy sigh rousing the dust on the table.

"I put Nadine in the car, and we followed her here. The Colton Bed & Breakfast, she'd said to me as she was leaving. That's where she was meeting her mistress. Of course, I knew where that was. I'd been coming to Camden for most of my life. I drove up and there was her car parked outside. For some reason, that's what set me off. I flew into a rage. How dare she leave us? I thought. How dare she assume that she could just drive out of our lives like that? Not after ten years together. Not after having a child together.

"I stormed in through that front door. Rizette greeted me and I demanded to know where my wife was. Maybe she could sense what was on my mind because she lied to me, said she didn't know. But I saw Salma's name in the guestbook. I saw her handwriting. That tiny signature was supposed to be the last clue before she disappeared." Laurel turns his gaze up toward the ceiling, pain across his face. "The innkeeper ran into the office closet, but she wasn't quick enough to lock it."

His fingers flex as if remembering the feeling of the door handle in his palms.

"I heard another door slam, and I ran out of the office. Only the bathroom door was closed. I knew someone had to be hiding inside. I screamed Salma's name but there came no answer. I pounded on the door, but they wouldn't let me in, so I kicked it open. Parrish was inside, cowering in the bathtub. He hadn't done anything. He was merely in the wrong place at the wrong time."

Tears are leaking out of Laurel's eyes now, but he doesn't show any signs he knows they're there. Brielle holds her breath, trying desperately not to make a sound. Nothing that might interrupt the man's confession. Inside, her stomach is roiling, filled with agony for the innocent lives lost in this house.

"And then I heard it. A loud creak from up above," he says, his voice deep and soft. "I ran up the stairs and checked the rooms, but they were all empty. Then I realized that none of the doors had made the sound when I'd entered them. They'd all been *silent*. I saw the hook in the corner and I looked up. She'd tried to make it look like nothing was out of the ordinary when she should've just taken the hook with her. Would've been easier for her too. I might've realized where she was, but I wouldn't have been able to enter.

"I lowered the ladder and climbed into the attic. There she was, cowering in the darkness, tears streaming down her beautiful face. Her fear and anger were so strong that I could feel them in my soul. 'You said I could go,' she screamed. But I'd changed my mind. That was an unacceptable way to leave. Not me. Not her daughter. Not for some queer whore she'd met in a bathroom. She's mine. I'm the one who loves her. *I'm* the one who promised to live my life by her side.

"I hit her, but I lost my balance and she escaped down the ladder. I followed. We struggled through the hall and down the stairs, where she managed to get away from me again. She tried to go out the front door, but I blocked it, so she ran to the window." He stops, heaving labored breaths as the tears continue to stream down his face. Then he leans forward to cover his face with his hands, sobbing into his palms as the moments tick by.

Brielle watches with an odd mixture of horror and satisfaction. He's confessed. He's admitted his wrongdoings. And though the truth is gruesome, it also brings closure.

"I don't know how long I stayed there cradling her body. What had once been my beautiful wife. She had betrayed me and yet I couldn't stop loving her. I didn't want to hurt her, but it was the only way I could make her stay. The only way to stop her from becoming a memory.

"When I heard sirens, I realized I was out of time. Someone must have alerted the police—perhaps Salma had used the house phone before I found her. I fled—"

"You abandoned Nadine?" Brielle chokes out, unable to stop herself. "After all that, you abandoned her at the scene of her mother's death?"

"I had no choice!" he hisses. "The police were here and I had no time to get her—to escape. I fled into the woods on foot. I left everything. It was my only option."

"And they never found you?"

He shakes his head adamantly, lips pressed together, face red.

"So why is your spirit here?"

"Because I came back," he says. "I lived in my parents' summer home. And any time someone came looking, I would hide in the basement. When all the police and the reporters and the nosy neighbors had gone, I came back here."

A smile breaks over his face. Tears and snot run rivers over his upper lip, and Brielle marvels at what a mess he has become.

"I returned because I still loved her," he says, whispering. "And she was here. I could see her. I could sense her. I had carved the life from her with my fingers and yet she persevered. But the only way we could be together was if I was here too. So I killed myself to ensure that she would never be without me again."

"Where's your body?" Brielle asks.

Laurel grins toothily—the look of a boy playing mischief. "So you can separate me and my Salma?" he says. "I won't let you do that."

"Tell me."

"You'd have better luck burning this whole place to the ground."

Brielle clenches her jaw, struggling to keep herself under control.

"You were sick," she says.

"Maybe," he replies, through his smile, his tears, and his mucus. "But I have what I wanted."

~

If she's going to break Salma's cycle of anguish, Brielle can think of only one remaining catalyst. As she drives away from the Garrick house, she dares to wonder if she could succeed tonight. She'll have to if she wants to make her mother's funeral in time. This morning, she'd been hoping Rhonda might bring resolution if she visited the former bed and breakfast to fulfill the promise made decades ago, but that's no longer a possibility.

She's halfway to Nadine's house when her phone rings. Brielle grunts in frustration, wondering what Kamnan can possibly want now. She's already volunteered to give a eulogy. What more assurances does he need that she'll be at the funeral? When she glances at the dashboard, however, she sees Vivian's name in bold white letters.

Wary, Brielle answers the call.

"Bri! Bri. Thank God you picked up," Vivian says through the speakers, harried and breathless.

"Vivian? What's wrong?"

For a long moment, there's nothing but several rushes of static. These are followed by a stifled cry.

"Vivian?" Brielle asks again, her worry growing.

"Brielle, I can't—I'm sorry. I'm so sorry. You were right." Her friend devolves into heavy sobs.

Alarmed, Brielle slows her driving. "Where are you? Do you need me to come—"

"No!" Vivian says. There's another rush of static. "Do you have a place I can go?"

"Yes, of course! I'm not there now, but I can—I'm staying in Camden. I can pick you up."

"No, please. I'm already in my car. Just send me the address."

Brielle pulls off to the side of the road, her heart hammering in her chest. She's so concerned by Vivian's sudden, fearful call that it takes her longer than it should to send the motel's location.

Twenty minutes later, Brielle finds herself back in her room.

Vivian arrives dressed in loose, ill-fitting clothing very contrary to what she'd worn on their lunch date. But she hasn't concealed the large bruise growing on the side of her face. The moment she removes her sunglasses, Brielle gasps.

"Viv," she whispers. And her friend devolves into tears.

They sit together on the bed, Brielle stroking Vivian's back comfortingly until she has calmed down enough to show her face again.

"He hadn't been like this in so long, I swear," she says, more to herself than to Brielle. "He hadn't had a drink in so long, hadn't gotten angry in forever."

"Viv, are you talking about Ben?"

Vivian's face is full of guilt.

"I thought you said you weren't together."

"I know. I'm sorry I lied to you. It's just…I knew what you would say if told you. I know he's made promises to me before, but this time it felt like he meant it. He'd made strides to better himself."

"It's hard not to believe in someone you've cared about for so long." Brielle sighs.

"I'm sorry I lied," Vivian repeats.

"You don't need to be sorry."

"I feel so stupid." Vivian leans over and grabs the tissue box from the bedside table. She takes a moment to compose herself, careful not to touch the violet bruise as she wipes at her eyes. "I'd gotten away from him. Two years we were apart. But I thought…I don't know, I guess I thought that maybe he *had* used that time to grow."

"Some people don't deserve the benefit of the doubt." Brielle has felt so many emotions today that, even though she's enraged by what Ben has done to Vivian, her anger is tempered by exhaustion.

"I wanted to believe him," Vivian says, shaking her head. "So bad, and I don't even know why. It's always the same thing and I always take him back. I feel like I'm stuck. Like I'm insane."

"You need to end it."

"Believe me, I want to. But it's not like last time—I'm not living with him. I can't just move out. I can't leave, I have my mom now. He knows where we live."

"We can get a restraining order," Brielle says, careful to let her friend know that she intends to help with the process.

"Will that work?"

"If it doesn't, you can have him arrested."

"Unless he…" Vivian's voice drifts away. "I don't want to consider that possibility."

"Or you move," Brielle says. "He's probably not going to take a break-up well."

Vivian nods. "You're probably right. But he did let me go once."

She doesn't need to finish her sentence. They both recognize that it didn't last.

"You can stay with me," Brielle says. "I was going to leave after finishing this job tonight, but I can extend—"

"No, please don't," Vivian says. "Not on account of me. If you don't mind me staying tonight, I need that. But I can't be away from my mom for too long."

"Where is she now?" Brielle asks.

"I took her to a friend's house. I figured it's best if we're not together right now. He might get violent, but it's only ever directed toward me." When she finishes saying this, silent tears start falling again. Brielle's heart aches. Vivian continues. "I didn't do anything to set him off. I didn't say anything…"

"It's not about you," Brielle says, trying not to sound like she's lecturing. She might be right, but this is neither the time nor the place. "It's about control. Knowing that he can do this to you and knowing you'll come back when he wants you. It's about feeling like you're his possession."

Vivian nods her head, but doesn't say anything this time. Instead, she gets up, walks across the room to throw away her used tissues, and sinks down into the chair. They sit in silence for several minutes. Brielle has known Vivian long enough to recognize that she's sorting things out in her head. Where others might try to fill the silence just to feel like they're doing something productive, she knows that this is the best time not to say anything at all. In another few minutes, Vivian will have made up her mind and will share her conclusions.

Almost as soon as Brielle thinks this, Vivian looks up at her.

"Thank you," she says. "I don't know what I would've done if you weren't here."

"Really, it's not a problem. I'm glad that I was." Brielle offers her a small smile.

"I won't go back to him. I won't let myself. I know I've said that before"—she pushes her hair back—"but I can't keep going through this."

"I believe in you," Brielle says.

Vivian lets out a long, slow breath, exhaling the pent-up fear inside her. She can't get rid of it completely—not yet, at least—but Brielle can see her relaxing. She's in a safe space.

"I'm fine now. Really. I think I'm just going to hang out here. You were in the middle of a job though."

"Viv, it's okay. I—"

"You were headed somewhere, I could tell. You had that determined voice when you answered the phone."

"The whole thing can wait for the night."

"No." Vivian pleads with her eyes, her hands clasped together in her lap. "Honestly, it would be great to be alone with myself for a little while. It's been so long since I've had that luxury. I'm not just saying that for your benefit. Really, I'm too selfish for that."

Brielle breaks into a wider smile, happy to hear her friend crack a joke, even if it is self-deprecating.

In truth, she needs to keep pursuing an end to the Garrick Estate haunting. She has a long drive to her mother's funeral. And if she can't resolve the spiritual turmoil in the old house tonight—well, she'll either have to give up or risk missing the funeral altogether. That's not something she wants to do.

"Are you sure you're okay here?"

"Yeah." Vivian waves a hand dismissively. "I can order delivery—you've got a laptop somewhere around here, right? I can binge *Mindhunter* until you get back."

"But—"

"I'm not going anywhere," Vivian says, and she stands, offering Brielle both of her hands.

Brielle takes them.

"Alright," she says. "Hopefully, if tonight is successful, I'll have closed this job. It's all really time sensitive, so it won't go on all night, trust me. If I'm not back by like ten…"

The sentence dies—she doesn't want to offer up a scenario like that, not when her friend is so vulnerable. Instead, she smiles again. "I'll be back by ten."

Vivian looks around before spotting Brielle's laptop half out of her bag. "I'll probably be asleep by then," she says.

Before the Window

The sun has set by the time Brielle reaches Nadine's house. She realizes quite suddenly that she hasn't had anything to eat all day besides her morning granola bar. Though her body is begging for sustenance, she ignores it. There isn't time for her to stop. Not now. Not when she could be so close to setting Salma and the other spirits free.

Nadine is not surprised to see Brielle there. She'd called ahead to let her know that her presence is needed tonight.

"We have to wait just a bit," Nadine says, checking her purse for some unknown item. "I called my usual babysitter. Luckily, she was available."

"Oh, I didn't realize," Brielle says, feeling somewhat guilty for the oversight. "Don't you leave every night?"

"I'm only gone twenty minutes, and Natalie's usually asleep by then."

"Right," Brielle says.

"She only lives ten minutes away, so it shouldn't be long."

Nadine finds what she was looking for, a ring of keys on a curled plastic lanyard.

"Are you going to be okay going in?" Brielle asks.

They lock eyes. In that instant, she detects uncertainty and fear. Regardless of how the woman answers, Brielle knows she will still need convincing when they get to the estate. It's understandable. Nadine has been going to the house every night for years without entering once. Calling upon someone to break your behavioral inertia can paralyze you. But Nadine will be convinced.

"I think so," she says. Her voice is small. "Yeah, I think so."

"Your father is in there too, you should know."

"Dad?" Nadine asks, shocked. "You didn't tell me…"

"I know," Brielle says. "I probably should have, but I wasn't sure at the time."

"When? But—"

Nadine lowers the purse on the table beside her, taking a minute for the information to process. Brielle can see a shimmer in her eyes. Perhaps this will be even more difficult than she'd expected.

"You should've told me," Nadine says, aggravated now.

"I'm sorry. I wasn't completely sure who he was at the time."

"Well, when you figured it out, I would've appreciated a call."

"I didn't have time," Brielle says. She shakes her head. "Things have been unfolding rather quickly. I was in Bangor this morning—"

Nadine isn't listening. She mumbles, "Dad's in there too."

A car door slams outside. The babysitter has arrived.

"I can explain everything on the ride over," Brielle says. Nadine locks eyes with her again, and this time there's a layer of wariness.

"I think that'd be best."

The doorbell rings, and she slides past Brielle to answer it.

~

In the car, Brielle tells Nadine everything she knows about her father: about his knowledge of Salma's secret affair, his surrender and subsequent decision to hunt Salma down and reclaim her, his uncontrolled murder of the three people at the Garrick house, and his suicidal return. Nadine listens in stunned silence, her expression—partially hidden by the night—a blank mask. When Brielle has finished, Nadine rests her chin on her closed fist, her elbow nestled into the armrest of the passenger door. From the reflection in the window, Brielle can see her watching the scenery roll by, the silhouettes of Camden cast dimly against the starry night.

"When you're a child," Nadine says, "everything feels as though it should be simple. You think to yourself, 'Mommy and Daddy left because they didn't want me. Grandma and Grandpa keep me because they love me.' The simple thoughts feel comforting and true."

"That doesn't mean they're wrong."

"It doesn't mean they're right either," Nadine says, looking over at Brielle. "To simplify emotions is to do them a disservice. You can love someone and also harm them, just as you can feel indifference toward someone and still treat them with care."

"But love shouldn't harm anyone."

"Love is very human, and no human is perfect. So why should love be?"

"Are you agreeing with your father that love made him kill your mother?"

"No," Nadine says, shaking her head. For a moment, the pain inside her peeks out. "All I'm saying is I don't doubt that he loved her just because he did a horrible thing with it."

"Your opinion wouldn't be popular with most people," Brielle says, turning into the driveway of the Garrick Estate. She'd left everything open and unlit, and without the glow of the lanterns, they might as well be driving into a void of darkness. "The type of love you describe isn't very beautiful."

"I think a lot of people have experienced pain on account of love," Nadine says. "So why should love be restricted to beauty?"

The car stops and she opens her door. Brielle follows her out into the chilly night, a cold wind playing through the air. The oak trees bordering the property creak, a chorus of vacant branches. Nadine stares up at the darkened house with a mixture of fear and apprehension. She's made it this far many times before, but Brielle is asking her to go further now—to face the spirits of her family and help them break their unending cycle.

"I can't do it," Nadine says, gripping the still-open door. "There has to be another way."

"You *can*," Brielle says. She walks around the car and places a hand on Nadine's back. "You *can* do this, believe me. It'll be difficult, but in the end, all of you will gain closure. Their spirits haunt more than this house."

The two women lock eyes, and Nadine frowns. "How do you know I'm the solution?"

"I've seen it a dozen times before."

"But what if you're wrong this time?"

"They're dead, Nadine. They can't do anything to you if you don't let them."

Nadine turns back to the house, her eyes lingering on the wide window. She usually waits here to see her mother on the other side of that glass. In the beginning, the vision struck fear in Nadine—the minutes leading up to it laced with apprehension. But it's been a long time since she felt that way. Lately, it's been more of a comfort, a necessity if she wants to sleep that night.

The fear is back.

"I can't force you to go inside," Brielle says gently, "but unless you want to keep returning here every night for the rest of your life, then you need to do this."

Nadine closes her eyes. She takes several deep breaths, perhaps sorting through the thoughts in her head, or maybe just listening to the sounds of the evening. Brielle gives her the space to do this, though she knows they're running out of time.

In the end, the car door shuts with a muffled thud.

"Okay," Nadine says.

Side by side, they walk up the stairs. At the top, Nadine takes out her key. The door swings open, and as they step across the threshold, the Garrick house sighs around them. The air is just as stale as ever, a musty odor still lingers, but everything feels different. More alive, somehow. More aware.

"Hello there." Rizette comes out of the office, taking in the sight of Nadine and Brielle with a vacant smile. "Who are you?"

"We're here to help," Brielle says, letting the door fall shut behind them.

"Checking in?"

Brielle frowns. "Not tonight."

"It's late," Rizette says, then lifts a hand to her forehead, suddenly worried. Recognition washes over her. "She's almost here."

"I know," Brielle says.

With a nod, Rizette retreats into her office again. Perhaps her spirit can feel the imminence of her departure. She seems more distant than usual. And the fact that she almost didn't recognize Brielle with Nadine there makes Brielle believe that they must be on the right track.

"Who was that?" Nadine asks.

"She was the innkeeper."

More footsteps. This time Parrish comes through the doorway out of the kitchen, intent on entering his guestroom. When he spies Brielle and the newcomer, he slows to a halt. "Who...?" he asks, his voice trailing off.

"I'm Nadine."

"Nadine," he repeats. Then he looks to Brielle expectantly.

"She's here to speak to her mother," Brielle explains.

Parrish nods. Without another word, he disappears into the bedroom.

"He was a guest at the time," Brielle says.

"My dad killed them both?"

"Unfortunately, yes."

"And they've been trapped here ever since?"

"All of them."

"Where is he?" Nadine asks. They haven't left the entryway.

"We won't be seeing him," Brielle says. "His spirit disappears earlier in the evening."

"Why?"

"Because he died at a different time than the others."

Nadine pauses, as if she means to ask more but isn't quite sure what. Brielle doesn't know how she would explain further. Ghosts seem to have their own rules. They come in all shapes and sizes, weak and strong. They may be powerful—deadly, even—or simply a shadow hiding in the corner that you're barely aware of. Some ghosts come every night to rob you of sleep, and some appear only every so often, visiting you in your best dreams. Brielle has seen ghosts that haunt people and ghosts that haunt places. And though they are untouchable by the living, the only thing that seems to bind them all is their ability to keep others in the past.

"It's almost time," Brielle says. "We should get in place."

"It's funny," Nadine says, stepping away from the front door at last. "I've spent so much time thinking about this place. I moved my family, my job. I expended so much energy and resources acquiring it, and this is the first time I've gone inside."

"Trauma will do that to you."

"The window is over here?" Nadine asks, following Brielle into the living room. As usual, everything is bathed in the pale glow of the moon: the dusty surfaces and faded rug, the aging leather upholstery and the abandoned books. All of it takes on an ethereal silver glow—fantastic and mystifying.

Nadine wanders over to the front of the room and looks down through the window at Brielle's car. Her mouth has become a straight line, her eyes glassy. Does she feel like the child waiting below, trapped and alone and confused?

The clock chimes—nine thirty—and the house is silent.

"Any minute now," Nadine says.

The telling creak from above, a drawn-out groan from the house. Brielle's ears ring in the quiet. The air is heavy and viscous. Nadine faces the room, the light of the moon at her back. Her elongated shadow stretches across the floor. Her face is a mask of pure terror. Her eyes search the dimness, unsure from where the vision will appear.

Brielle doesn't dare to breathe, afraid to relax even the tiniest bit. She doesn't want to be the one to break the stillness. But where is Salma's ghost? She can't remember there being this long of a gap between the attic door opening and her appearance in the living room.

"Is she—" Nadine begins, but then the sofa slides several inches backward.

Nadine looks to Brielle.

"She knows you're here," Brielle says, perhaps unnecessarily, but in her experience, people encountering spirits for the first time are not always thinking critically.

"Is she angry?" Nadine whispers.

"I can't tell," Brielle says. Her senses have become a conflicting array.

In the next instant, there's movement everywhere. Anything that is not secured to the floor of the living room is pushed unceremoniously against the wall opposite the window. The bookshelves, the door into the dining area—all of it is blocked by the shifting furniture. As the rug is sent sailing, the dark wooden floor is revealed, bathed in silver light.

Brielle thinks she hears an exclamation, an involuntary gasp. But she cannot see anyone besides Nadine. The woman looks utterly terrified now, clutching her chest, displayed in the bay window like prey. On the floor, beneath where the rug had been, long red streaks are revealed mere feet from her. She stares down at them, mouth open in a silent scream.

"Nadine," Brielle says, trying to sound calmer than she is. "Get away from the window."

But the woman doesn't seem to hear her. She stares down at the bloody marks, chest heaving beneath her palms.

"Nadine."

But it's no use.

A cloud moves in front of the moon. The room dims to almost nothing, the silver, ethereal light stolen from them. Shadows grow, crawling out of the dark corners to claim the empty space.

Out of the corner of her eyes, Brielle catches movement. She turns her head in time to see the thin figure of a woman in a pale dress step through the open doorway. Her pace is even and unhurried. Her hair is dark and tattered. And she walks directly toward Nadine.

"Salma," Brielle calls out, hoping to distract the ghost. Nadine is still fixated on the blood stains, but when she hears her mother's name, she too looks and sees the ghost entering the living room. "Salma Toren!"

The spirit slows to a halt, her tattered dress hanging from her withered limbs in rags. It's hard to make out anything of her in the dark beside her white dress, but Brielle remembers the way she looked. Every visible inch of her skin purple and rotten. She remembers the blood staining her clothes. The look of agony on her face as she screamed.

"Your daughter is here," she says, and points toward the window. "That's Nadine. Your little girl."

"It's true, Mom," Nadine says, suddenly sounding years younger as she pleads for her mother's recognition. "It's me. I'm here."

The ghost turns her head again, looking from Brielle to Nadine. It's still too dark to see anything other than the rotation of her dress, but the movement is clear.

The house remains still, holding its breath as it seemed to do when Brielle was in the attic, when it wanted her to find the suitcase.

Even the sounds from outside—the wind, the rustle of the tree branches—are gone. Leaving a void where just the three souls exist.

"You've been here for so long," Nadine says, her voice still very small. "It's been thirty years since you left."

At this, a loud crack rattles the darkness. Brielle feels the house judder, the floor shifting beneath her feet. She stumbles to the wall closest to her and braces herself against it.

"I know why you did what you did," Nadine continues. "I know why you left. You were in love. Brielle told me about the letters. About how you were going to leave Portland and start a new life with Rhonda. I know."

More movement, this time from above. Shifting furniture. Water rushing through the old pipes, cascading through the house like a violent pulse.

"I know you weren't dealt the greatest lot in life, Mom," Nadine continues. With each word, her voice grows stronger. The house might appear angry, but none of its aggression has come close to hurting her. It's as though, even through the turmoil, it still wants to hear what she has to say. "You felt forced to live a lie, forced into a box that wasn't you. Back then, people were less accepting. You didn't want to marry a man. You didn't even want me. You never wanted me."

The doors shake, the knobs rattle.

Brielle can hear the hurt in Nadine's words. The underlying pain that has persisted through her years of wondering. She speaks louder, determined that her words be heard above the chaos.

"Even after you had me, you didn't want me."

There's a howling in the chimney, and suddenly the room is full of blustering winds that swirl in a violent tornado. Brielle presses herself further against the wall, straining her eyes against the darkness and the gusts to watch the scene unfold. But Salma has disappeared into the tornado, the faint image of her white dress vanished.

"That's fine if you didn't want a child, but I *was* your child. You had me, and you shouldn't have left me like that. Neither of you should've left me." Nadine is shouting now, calling into the storm as she stands in the shallow alcove. "You wouldn't have me. Dad wouldn't have me. Grandma and Grandpa only took me in because they had no choice. I have felt so unwanted all my life!"

The windows are rattling now, chattering like teeth. Brielle is certain that at any moment the house will collapse and they'll be lost in a pile of rubble. There is too much anger here, too much hurt, too much sadness.

"But you know what?" Nadine screams. "I have never hated you. Do you hear that? I was hurt by what happened, *but I have never blamed you!*"

Everything goes still at once. The rushing water ceases, the gusting winds fade, dropping dust and pages torn from dislodged books. The doors no longer tremble, and their knobs stop twisting. Even the windows stop their chatter, though the largest pane behind Nadine has cracked.

Nadine is out of breath, eyes darting around the room. But though the commotion has settled, Salma's ghost remains invisible.

"Most of us are just doing the best we can with the circumstances we're given. In a world where you were accepted, you never would've felt the pressure to have me. You might've fallen in love with Rhonda and been okay." Nadine steps away from the window, holding out her hands as if maybe she can feel her way to her mother. Some of the moonlight has trickled back into the room. Enough that Brielle can see the tears in her eyes. "You may not have been perfect, but I *don't* think you were a terrible person, Mom. I don't. I forgive you. But more than that, I accept you for who you were."

The light increases, and with it, Salma reappears. She stands in the center of the wide window, where she has appeared every evening since the night she died. But rather than staring out at the world and the life that was taken from her, she is facing inward at the daughter who has come to offer acceptance. Her face, her skin, her tattered and bloodied dress look the same as they did—a gruesome reminder of her fate—but she's not screaming or angry. Instead, she appears to breathe—calm, full breaths.

Spotting her, Nadine turns and tries to reach her mother, but the woman disappears before she can get to her, fading into the silvery light like a cloud passing over the moon. Instead, Nadine's hands graze the cracked window.

"Is she gone?" Nadine asks, tears running down her face. "Did it work?"

"I think so," Brielle says, noticing that she doesn't feel the presence of the house any longer. It's just a house, after all—made of wood, and nails, and all other manner of inanimate things. If she had to bet, she would guess that all the other spirits have gone as well. "How did you know what to say?"

"I didn't, but it's what I've been wanting to tell her for years," Nadine says. She smiles, wiping away her tears. "And to think I could've come in here at any point."

"You can't understand anything without knowing the truth." Nadine nods.

And then a scream of rage cuts through the darkness.

"*No!*"

Brielle's head whips around. The voice is coming from the blocked doorway into the dining room. The shifted furniture moves slightly.

"How dare you! You had no right!"

An end table goes tumbling, and then an arm reaches out of a gap and wraps around a bookshelf, shoving it aside.

"That was *my* wife," Laurel says, emerging from the shadows.

"She's gone, Laurel. It's over," Brielle says sternly. She'd thought for sure all the other ghosts would've gone.

"Dad?" Nadine says.

Rage burns in Laurel's eyes. His fists are clenched, veins pulsing in his arms and his neck. At once, Brielle is aware of the same rage that had consumed him the night he committed the murders. Her heart begins hammering in her chest; a sensation like a cold droplet of water runs down her spine. This is wrong.

"Dad? You look different," Nadine says. "Older."

"He isn't a ghost," Brielle says. And then, "Run."

She turns on her heel, ready to sprint for the door, but before she and Nadine can move, Laurel has darted forward. He seizes Nadine around the throat and slams her against the window. The glass shatters, raining down in a mass of shards. Nadine lets out a choked scream. Cold air fills the room again, blowing in through the open window frame.

Laurel releases Nadine and she slumps to the ground, gasping for air.

Face alight with demonic fury, he rounds on Brielle. His right hand is coated with blood.

"*You fucking whore,*" he hisses at her. "She was my wife. How dare you!"

"She was dead," Brielle says. She tries to search for a weapon without taking her eyes off of him, feeling along the wall.

"Even so, I still had her. She was still here," Laurel says, hands balled into fists again. "And you took her away from me! Everyone is always trying to take her away from me."

"Laurel, you *killed* her!"

"So she couldn't leave!" He screams the words like an animal roaring in agony. "She wasn't going to give me a chance. I alone appreciated how perfect and beautiful she was. All I ever wanted was to make her happy."

"But you couldn't!" Brielle curses the lump rising in her throat. Now is not the time to cry. "You weren't what she wanted. You were part of the problem."

"I gave her *everything*."

They are both out of breath now from shouting. Nadine still has not stirred. Brielle thinks she can see a puddle of blood beneath her. *Please don't be dead.*

"No amount of desire can guarantee an outcome," Brielle mutters. Then, louder, "She never loved you, Laurel. And nothing you could do would've changed that."

The man lunges forward, letting out a guttural cry that chills Brielle to the bone. Her hand closes around something—the base of a table lamp—and she hurls it at him. He bats it out the air as she sprints for the doorway. Their footfalls drum on the floor, the noise echoing through the empty house. Brielle can see the front door, the colored glass windows beckoning to her like a signal in the darkness. Her arms pump at her sides. Mere feet away.

Suddenly, she's lifted off the ground and thrown backward. For a brief moment, she sails weightless through the air. Then she crashes to the floor, her back colliding with the hardwood. Brielle lets out a grunt as the wind is knocked from her. Stars explode before her eyes.

"I thought I could scare you away with blood," Laurel growls. His knees crash down on either side of her, pinning Brielle to the floor. Her vision is still swimming, but she swings a fist with all her might. It collides with something hard—maybe his jaw—and Laurel recoils but doesn't move away. "I should've known it wouldn't be enough. Especially once I caught you in the attic with her belongings."

"You put the deer on my car," Brielle wheezes, still trying to get air back in her lungs. "You should've thought about your daughter. You still had Nadine! You abandoned her."

"I had to! Once my wife was dead, I never would've been allowed to keep her."

"She needed you!" Brielle shouts. As he reaches for her throat, she grabs him by the wrists. Though she manages to keep him from crushing her windpipe, he's strong. She won't be able to hold him back for long. "She needed you to be her support. You could've been each other's support!"

"Salma was her mother," Laurel snarls, leaning all his weight forward. His fingers curl around Brielle's throat, eager to choke the life out of her. As the pressure builds, Brielle's vision tunnels. The darkness and the shadows twist together, distorting Laurel's shape. "She gave birth to her. She needed to be there to raise her!"

A sudden crash in the dark. Laurel's eyes go wide, and his strength extinguishes. The force of the blow carries him sideways, and he collapses to the floor in a heap beside Brielle.

She gasps as air returns to her, devolving into dry, heaving coughs and clutching at her own throat. Nadine is standing above her, holding the neck of a shattered vase. Blood is running down her face, but she doesn't seem to notice. It heightens the expression of unbridled fury there. The disgust. "I needed to be wanted," she says, staring down at her unconscious father. "I needed a home."

Her thrumming heart beating in her ears, Brielle lays her head back on the ground. The world fades in and out of darkness—a disorienting succession of moments. As she wills her breath to slow, the images steady themselves and suddenly living room is suddenly awash in red and blue flashing lights from the driveway below. She doesn't wonder why the police are here—she doesn't have the mental capacity at the moment. Instead, she closes her eyes and listens to the sirens and wind coming through the wide window.

ELEGY FOR TWO

Brielle stands in the vestibule, the muffled congregation a barely audible hum beyond the closed door. Light streams through the rose-glass window, dying the air a delicate pink. Alone in the tiny room, she turns on the spot, acknowledging the religious iconography displayed on the walls that were once so familiar to her. In the miniscule closet are hung dozens of robes as well as a variety of colored cords. Decades ago, she would've come storming in here, aggravated by having to be an altar server—one of the youths who aid the priest throughout the ceremony—and yet secretly pleased by her sense of importance. Despite her reluctance, the ceremony hinged on her participation. The egotism makes her smirk now.

The door opens, momentarily filling the vestibule with the chatter from outside. The church must be full of people come to see her mother off. Fitting. Her mother had many friends in life.

Kamnan steps inside and shuts the door behind him, reducing the noise to a muffled hum again. He smiles sadly at his sister, and they embrace.

"Brielle, it's good to see you," he says, and takes a seat against one of the walls. Brielle feels an instinctual reaction to stop him— that's the priest's chair. But of course he wouldn't know; he was never an altar server. The reaction is silly too, she reflects. The priest isn't here.

"It's good to see you too," Brielle says. They are both dressed all in black.

"Your last job went alright then?" he asks.

"It was successful."

"You were able to save them?"

Brielle nods. "Coincidentally, I was saved as well."

"Oh?" Kam grins. "By a ghost?"

"No. By Vivian."

"She was with you?"

"Yeah, she stayed in my motel room for one night while I resolved the case. When I didn't return when I said I would, she called the police. Nadine was just about to leave for help when they arrived."

"Nadine?"

"My contact."

Kam raises an eyebrow. "Is this something I'm going to read about in the news?"

"Maybe, but probably not." Brielle shrugs. "It's a pretty small town."

Not thinking, she brushes her hair back from her shoulder and immediately regrets the action when Kam spies the bruises along the side of her neck.

"Bri!" he gasps.

"It's fine. I'm fine," Brielle says, hurriedly sweeping the hair back into place.

"I thought you said it went alright?"

"I said it was successful." She shrugs.

"How did you get that then?"

She crosses her arms over her chest. "I thought one of the people involved was a ghost. But he was only pretending—living in one of the rooms and climbing down from the window to get food."

"Bri!" Kam exclaims. They both look to the door leading out into the church, wondering if anyone had heard him. But the hum of chatter continues. He turns back to his sister. "I thought you could tell that sort of thing."

"I know, I know. I just—I took the job after Mom died to distract myself, but I couldn't focus."

"Some things you can't run away from," he says gently.

Brielle wants to tell him he doesn't know how right he is, but she doesn't. Instead, she simply nods.

"How long had he been hiding there?"

"Almost thirty years," Brielle says. "Apparently, there was a lot of money hidden in the basement."

Kam lets out a low whistle. "You run into some ridiculous things. You need to be careful."

"I might take a break after this one."

"Well, I'm glad you're safe."

He kneads his temples with his fingers. Then crosses his legs and leans back against the wall beneath the window. For a moment, Brielle can see how tired her brother is. He looks older than when she last saw him, even though it was only a couple weeks ago. His smile is genuine, but less lively than it used to be. Dealing with the aftermath of their mother's death has been hard on him, and she appreciates Kam for taking on all the responsibilities that followed.

Part of her feels guilt for having left, but he's so much better at that sort of thing. And she would've only gotten in the way.

"How are you doing?" he asks gently.

"Okay," Brielle says. She realizes that she's wringing her hands together and stops. Instead, she grabs something hanging on the wall: a tool used to light or extinguish the candles on the altar. One side is shaped like a bell, while the other is a spout with an inch or so of white wick poking out of it. "I've been thinking a lot lately," she says, turning the tool over in her hands. "Memories and all that."

"Yeah, I know what you mean," Kam says. "I think my mind has done more remembering this past week than in all the years of my life combined. Like I've been trying to recall every single detail of our time with her. Do you remember at family parties, when we used to sit outside with our cousins and try to tell each other's parents apart by their laughs?"

"Mom's was always the easiest to pick out."

"Because it was the loudest."

They both smile.

Kam says, "I stayed with Dad at the house. He had me help him with her closet. We put plastic over all her clothes so they wouldn't get ruined. I didn't want to ask how long he planned to keep them there. I didn't have the heart."

"There's no rush."

"I know," Kam says, shaking his head. "It's just difficult. There's so much of her lingering in that house. It's impossible to avoid. I was sitting in the backyard and couldn't help noticing all the wind ornaments everywhere. I never noticed how many there were until that moment."

"Her favorite was the blue-and-green one outside the kitchen," Brielle whispers. She sighs, hating herself for needing to say what comes next. "I haven't just been remembering though. I've been coming to terms with things that I've always kept at arm's length."

Kam watches her but says nothing, his hands folded in his lap.

"For a long time, I was afraid of Mom," she says.

"Bri—"

"You were too. Don't deny it," Brielle pleads. "We have to talk about it, Kam. I know it's difficult, but it needs to be said."

"Yeah, she had a bad temper, but that's—I mean, our parents were just strict."

"Dad never did some of the things she did. Remember how she would grab me by my hair?"

Her brother says nothing, but he looks away, eyes downcast.

"I saw her do the same to you more than once," Brielle says. Her voice is low, perhaps because she doesn't want to risk anyone overhearing, but maybe also because if she speaks too loudly he will reject the conversation altogether. "It didn't happen all the time, but she had anger issues and I'm tired of denying it—to myself and to you."

"Are you saying she was an awful person?"

"No, I'm not." Brielle sets the extinguisher down, willing herself to stay calm. She drops into the only other chair in the room—the one meant for the altar server—and returns to wringing her hands. "And I think that's what messed me up for so long. She could be loving and sweet and thoughtful, and would've fought until the end to protect us, but she had these moments of—of violence that I didn't know what to do with. I couldn't process."

"Discipline was different back then."

"Kam. There's a difference between a spanking and pushing someone to the ground. And I realize she wasn't beating us—we never bruised or bled—but there was a definite line she crossed."

Brielle can see him struggling. The fight he's having in his head now is the one she's been having for several years. One that she never wanted to have because it threatened to taint all the good childhood memories she held dear. The clock ticks ever closer to the start of the funeral, but it's too late now to change course. With a simmering guilt, Brielle watches the first tears spill from her brother's eyes.

"You know," he says, "I only learned that Grandpa used to get violent a couple years ago?"

Nobody had told Brielle that.

"Mom let it slip in the most subtle way. I don't even think she meant to tell me. It just came out." He wipes at one eye, looking briefly at the moisture on his fingers. "I was so conflicted because suddenly all my memories of Grandpa seemed fake. How could he have been the person I loved *and* the person who hurt her? And how could she continue to talk about loving him when he'd been capable of that? It didn't make sense."

Brielle shakes her head. "I didn't know."

"I didn't want to tell you," Kam admits. "Not after how it changed my opinion of Grandpa—my memories."

"That's one of the main reasons I was so hesitant to come today," Brielle says. In the pink light streaming through the stained window, she can see dust floating about. The clock continues its steady ticking. The hum of distant conversation persists. "Everyone is so afraid to speak ill of the dead that the deceased become glorified paintings of themselves. These impossibly perfect ghosts that we cling to. It dehumanizes them. Destroys their actual memory. Takes away the complexities that made them who they were. I didn't want to create a fictional account of my mom for everyone else to fawn over. How am I supposed to tell them that the most meaningful memory I have is when she apologized to me if I can't also tell them that she could be abusive? She wasn't all bad, but neither was she all good. And our relationship was rocky and complicated and took some mending because it could be tumultuous as well as sweet. Yes, I forgave her, but it took me *so many years* to reconcile with the past. I am still reconciling with the past."

Brielle's heart aches. Her eyes burn from crying. But she's grateful for this moment alone with her brother, grateful to be away from the dozens—possibly hundreds—of people gathered in the church. She hadn't known they'd be having this conversation today, but it's one she's needed for a very long time.

"You know I was afraid to have kids because I thought I would hurt them?" Brielle says when she's calmed down enough to speak again. "I thought pain was a never-ending cycle and we were bound to keep passing it along from one person to another." She scoffs. "That was without even knowing about Grandpa."

"Do you still believe that?" Kam asks.

"I don't know," Brielle admits. "I really don't know."

Kam stands and walks over to her. He kneels by her side and takes one of her hands in his. Brielle might've normally pulled away, unused to such blatant and vulnerable displays of familial affection, but she allows it.

"If you could say exactly what you want to say without the expectations and opinions of everyone out there," Kam says, "what would it be?"

At first, Brielle feels awkward answering his question—a private eulogy for the two of them feels silly. But why should it? Every person is slightly different in the eyes of those who know them. No one else experienced their mother in the same way as Kamnan and Brielle. Not even their father, though he lived under the same roof.

"Mom was challenging," Brielle says. Her voice is hoarse from crying, so she clears her throat. "She was loving, attentive, and had a not-so-secret sweet tooth. But she was also strict, stubborn, and at times, extremely short-tempered."

Kam nods silently, his grip on her hand tightening.

"I spent a lot of my life confused about how I felt about her. I loved her, yes, but was I allowed to love someone who had hurt me before? If I loved her, how was I supposed to forget what she'd done in her worst moments?" Brielle takes a deep breath. "But that was the wrong way to think about it.

"I don't think we should remember people for being purely good or purely bad. Nobody is exactly one or the other. I think our overall judgment should be whether they opened themselves to positive change when their shortcomings were brought to light. Whether the good they did outweighs the bad.

"That threshold is going to be different for each person, and that's okay. We aren't all going to come to a consensus. Recognizing that there can be room for growth, to make amends, is one of the hardest struggles. For yourself and for other people."

The congregation is beginning to quiet. People are taking their seats, which means the priest has probably arrived. He's probably waiting at the back of the church for Kam and Brielle to appear before starting the ceremony.

"My mother came to me and apologized," Brielle says. "This was years after the last incident. By then, I'd already decided to forgive but not forget. Once I knew what she'd come to do, it felt like she was opening an old wound. Did I really need to revisit the worst of her? But until that conversation, I didn't realize how much I needed that apology. Actions are the bulk of healing, but words are the stitches that close the wound.

"I loved my mom and I still love my mom—all the more for her ability to change."

The warmth of her brother's hands is comforting. Delicate. Brielle breathes slowly in and out. And though it aches, she knows her heart is beating. In this moment, she finds that she is both profoundly sad and profoundly aware that she's alive.

How strange that one should be a prerequisite for the other.

RD Pires was born and raised in Northern California, where he developed his love for writing at a young age. He is the author of the novel A Vast, Untethered Ocean and the short story collection A Sky Littered With Stories. He currently lives in Sacramento with his husband.

CPSIA information can be obtained
at www.ICGtesting.com
Printed in the USA
LVHW050018210123
737602LV00004B/190